Tell No Man

T.J. Tranchell

Last Days Books

Email the author at: tj.tranchell@gmail.com

Website: www.tjtranchell.net
Facebook: www.facebook.com/TJTranchell

"Tell No Man" Printing History
Last Days Books paperback edition February 2021

This is a work of fiction. Names, characters, places, and incidents either are the product of the author's imagination or are used fictitiously. Any resemblance to actual persons, living or dead, events, business establishments, or locales is entirely coincidental.

ISBN:978-0-578-82759-9

Printed in the United States of America
Www.tjtranchell.net

Praise for...

Cry Down Dark:

"This is the kind of knife-edge story that will keep you up at night, startling at every noise." — *New York Times*

Asleep in the Nightmare Room:

"If you enjoy horror but want to try something a little different, I definitely recommend this inspired, personal, and thought provoking collection."

— Jennifer Soucy, author of *Demon in Me, The Night She Fell,* and *Clementine's Awakening*

The Private Lives of Nightmares:

"Tranchell flaunts his literary chops once more with further proof of both his fiction and nonfiction abilities."

— Michelle von Eschen, author of *Mistakes I Made During the Zombie Apocalypse, When You Find Out What You're Made Of,* and *Last Night While You Were Sleeping*

Tell No Man:

"*It's* creepy, fast, and the right kind of gory."

— Gabino Iglesias, author of *Zero Saints* and *Coyote Songs*

For

Mom

Grateful acknowledgment to Joshua Demarest, who published what is now the prologue "Chile" of TELL NO MAN in Gallows Hill Issue 1, Oct. 2017.

THANK YOU

Thank to everyone who helped make this book possible. My early readers who helped with the Spanish were Luis Torres and Dalyn Erekson. Vera Hamilton Forsythe provided valuable insight as I wrote the final chapters. Sadie Moore helped make sure Maddie Smith sounded and behaved like a woman. Ryan Bailey made sure everything else made sense.

Gabino Iglesias edited the novel once I decided to self-publish it and the book is much better because of him.

A huge thank you to all the writers and readers who encouraged me to take charge of my fate with this book: Joe Johnson, Michelle Kilmer, Jonathan Lambert, Rob Erekson, Linsey Knerl, Jennifer Soucy, Jay Bower, Scott J. Moses, Chip Erekson, Thom Carnell, Molly Mooney, Pam Weiss, Brianna Johnson, Heather Perkins, Jake Stanton, Amanda Roberts, Elaina Johnson, Eric Morgret, and so many more.

To Dr. Stephen Taysom, author of "'Satan Mourns Naked upon the Earth': Locating Mormon Possession and Exorcism Rituals in the American Religious Landscape, 1830-1977." This book took on a new and more valid life once I found Dr. Taysom's work.

In addition, William Peter Blatty's *The Exorcist*, Paul Tremblay's *A Head Full of Ghosts*, and Grady Hendrix's *My Best Friend's Exorcism* were the novels I read while writing. Father Gabriele Amorth's *An Exorcist Tells His Story*, Malachi Martin's *Hostage to the Devil*, and M. Scott Peck, M.D.'s *A Glimpse of the Devil* were the nonfiction books I read. Scott Derrickson's films *The Exorcism of Emily Rose* and *Deliver Us from Evil* were also vital.

Charity Becker continues to rock.

The excitement from my son Clark regarding my writing keeps me going and I wouldn't be the same person without him.

For my mom DeeAnna and my sister Leslie, you were on my mind the most while writing this.

And finally, my wife Savannah, who didn't even blink when I said I was thinking of self-publishing this book after going through one publisher and sending out again. If you see her, tell her thank you. This book wouldn't be in your hands without her support.

Table of Contents

Forward

I love horror. I love horror short stories and novels. I love horror poetry. Give me all your zombies, werewolves, ghosts, and witches. Give me your slashers and kaiju. Gothic, modern, American, and worldwide; I love it all.

Second to ghost stories, I love possession stories. Demons infesting every day people. Usually people that didn't ask for it, or made some stupid mistake that invited evil into their lives.

Walked in on a pagan ritual in the woods and the participants weren't happy about it? You have a demon.

Played with a speaking board, even one of those "games" you can buy at the local big box store? You have a demon, too.

In many ways, possession is like the sci-fi movies featuring artificial intelligences that take over your house. You didn't want to clean your bathroom and now the disembodied voice of Pierce Brosnan is trying to kill your husband. Bring that to today and you wanted Alexa to pick a playlist and turn your lights off. What do you think is going to happen next?

Mess with Ouija and bad things are coming up. You brought that on yourself.

I hear many people say the same thing about writing a book like this. That I'm inviting—and therefore inviting you, too—evil upon myself. I don't believe that. I'm of the Scott

Derrickson school of thought. Paraphrasing the director, he said that horror is the best place for a religious person because it is the genre in which the battle between good and evil is right up front. Three of Derrickson's films--"The Exorcism of Emily Rose," "Deliver Us From Evil," and "Sinister" were influences here. And then you'll see my biggest problem.

None of those movies, and none of the literature in print or film, talked about the demons of the faith I grew up with: Mormonism.

So I had to do it and here it is. I'll talk more about that when you finish reading this book. Let me say now that this book is quite personal (if you've read my previous work, you know that's true of everything I write), and one of the most difficult things I've written. The difference is that I was able to write it much faster than "Cry Down Dark" and my hope is that I can keep up that pace.

My hope with this book is that, if you are a person of faith, you will see that horror can be for you, too. And if you are not a person of faith, well, you'll still enjoy it. This story is still for you.

So here we go, once more to a small Utah town that should seem familiar. It's like you've been there before.

It's like home.

No, it is home.

Part One:
Mountains

And Jesus saith unto him, "See thou tell no man; but go thy way,
shew thyself to the priest, and offer the gift that Moses
commanded, for a testimony unto them."
Matthew 8:4, King James Bible

Chile

Elder Blaine Griffen held the small, plastic vial of oil between his fingers, ready to twist the lid off and drip the contents onto the head of the young Chilean mother sitting before him. Elder Rey Montoya, Griffen's junior companion, stood still, waiting for Griffen to pour the oil before placing his hands on the mother's head.

"¿Hermana Molina, estás lista?" Elder Griffen said. After more than a year in the mission field, the Spanish language came quickly to him, just as it would during the prayer he was about to speak. He spun the lid off the vial and lifted it over Sister Molina's head. A few drops of the consecrated oil settled in Sister Molina's dark hair. Elder Griffen put the lid back on the bottle and nodded at Elder Montoya to join him.

The woman's family watched as the missionaries prepared to give her a blessing. Her husband held their young child and Sister Molina held her stomach to hold back the pains she still felt months after giving birth.

The two young men had been visiting the Molinas for about five months, just before the birth of Vicente, their son. Montoya had only been in the field for a month and had been Griffen's companion for a week when they met the Molinas. Serving in Chile had been difficult for them, but with the

15

Santiago temple nearing dedication, the people of the city and the small villages they served seemed more open to hearing the message of Jesus.

For Griffen, being a Mormon was all he had ever known. Home was thousands of miles away in Blackhawk, Utah, and he had not planned his life beyond his two years as an LDS missionary. Teaching people about Christ in Chile had been a challenge because most of the people already knew who Jesus was. Catholic iconography dominated the area—even the name of the city their mission was based in had Catholic roots.

Montoya, a year younger than Griffen, had come to the mission field from New Mexico. He was more familiar with Catholicism and his grandmother—his abuela, a word Griffen adored—still spoke of the saints she had left behind in Guadalupe. She traded holy virgins and patrons for Joseph Smith and a story she could relate to, claiming to have seen Jesus on the day her husband died crossing the border.

With the elders' hands placed gently atop Sister Molina's head, Elder Griffen began the prayer he had practiced in his head since he was first ordained to the Melchizedek Priesthood of the Church of Jesus Christ of Latter-day Saints.

"Sister Consuela González Molina, by the authority of the Melchizedek Priesthood, we anoint you with oil that has been set apart for blessing the sick and afflicted in the name of Jesus Christ. Amen."

It was short, but Elder Griffen felt compelled to let Elder Montoya do the actual blessing part. Montoya's Spanish was more fluid and contained notes of sincerity Griffen struggled with. He thought Sister Molina's husband would appreciate hearing a native speaker bless his suffering wife.

"Sister Consuela González Molina, by the authority of the Melchizedek Priesthood which we hold, we seal the anointing and ask Our Heavenly Father to place his healing touch upon your body, your mind, and your spirit.

"The pains in your stomach from bringing another of the Lord's children into the world are horrible and we ask the Lord that the pain be taken from you. We ask that the cause of the pain be identified and that if further medical treatment be needed that such will be provided.

"Sister Molina, you are a gift to this world, one of our Heavenly Father's precious children. You are a gift to your husband and to the son he holds in his arms. Your pain and suffering are great, Heavenly Father and His son know. Through this blessing, we ask that you be comforted in the love of Jesus Christ, our savior.

"Sister, be blessed and always remember the Lord's love for you.

"We pray this in the name of Jesus Christ. Amen."

The young men's hands lingered over Sister Molina's hair for just a moment.

Then the ground began to tremble.

Sister Molina sat up, reaching for her baby. She didn't express any of the pain that had plagued her since the birth of her child. Her husband wrapped his arms around her as she clutched young Vicente to her bosom. Brother Molina spoke rapidly, telling the elders they should take shelter within the posts of the front door of the shack as they cowered under similar posts between the main room and a small kitchen.

The tremors were not the worst either of the elders had experienced during their time in Santiago. They smiled at each other, neither needing to speak aloud about how swiftly Sister Molina moved following her blessing. They shook hands as the quake subsided.

Screams came rolling down the street, getting louder as they got closer to the Molina home.

"¿Ven a mis hermanos?" a strong but worried voice cried.

"Do you think he's looking for us?" Elder Montoya asked his companion.

"He might be, but he sounds like he needs help, so we should find out," Elder Griffen said. The two men said their goodbyes, dusted off their white shirts, straightened their ties, and went outside.

A man holding his arms out saw them and began running. "Hermanos, ayúdenme. Él la tiene. Él la tiene pos."

"Who has her? Who?" Elder Griffen said as he gripped the man's shoulders. "What can we do?"

"¡Él diablo pos! Él la tiene cachaí. El diablo tiene a mi hija."

The devil has my daughter.

***

The young men jumped over ever-growing piles of rubble as they followed the distraught man back to his home. Other cries for help hit their ears but they ignored them for now, hoping maybe this was something other than what the man said.

Soon, they reached a home that looked just like all the others on the street: a mix of loose bricks and sheets of tin, remnants of an older home built upon with materials that could be easily scavenged from construction near the city's center. And like most of the other homes the elders passed, this one had a huddled family outside of it.

Instead of looking around at the damage to other homes, these four bodies stood close to each other, muffling the sounds of weeping that could have come from one or all of them. Shrouds of dark cloth hung from each head as if they were already mourning a family member who had died in the earthquake that stopped less than fifteen minutes prior.

Montoya approached the group and the weeping became words:

"Padre nuestro
Que estás en los cielos.

Santificado sea tu nombre.

Venga a nosotros tu reino…"

"They are praying the Lord's prayer," Montoya said to Griffen. "Something bad happened in there."

Griffen could see rapid movements in the spaces between the four people. Hands blurred from forehead to chest, from shoulder to shoulder.

"Let's see what he needs," Griffen said. The man they followed opened the door and waved them inside.

The light from outside stopped at the door jamb. The darkness enveloped Montoya and Griffen even as they peered over their shoulders at the afternoon glow of the street. The four cloaked figures remained outside, and the door soon closed upon them. The man grabbed each of the missionaries by the arm and pulled them forward. Another door opened and soon the two men stood in a room filled with darkness and a stench like that of a sewer running beneath a slaughterhouse. The smell did not emanate from above or below but rather from a corner deeper in the room. The distance felt much farther to Montoya than the size of the shack led him to believe possible. He stared into the corner, the lack of light and the heavy smells pounding into him.

Something the size of a rat moved in front of them. Montoya felt Griffen freeze at the sign of motion. Montoya, however, continued forward.

"No te acerques. El diablo te agarrará, a ti también," the man whispered.

"He's right, Montoya," Griffen said, dropping his Spanish for the first time in months. "Let's not get too close until we know what's going on."

But Montoya continued walking toward the corner. He could feel pain pulsing from the spot where he saw movement. "We need to help her," he said, still using the Spanish that flowed through his mind and blood.

"You can't help her, you pig," said a throaty voice in

English from the darkness. "She belongs to me and I'm taking her to Hell."

From behind him, Montoya heard the man asking Griffen what the voice had said. The man didn't know English, yet somehow his daughter spoke the language perfectly and with no accent.

As Griffen held the man, trying to comfort him, Montoya turned back to the corner and stepped forward. His feet bumped a mattress and he took a step back, then kicked out to find the mattress again. Instead of kicking the mattress, his foot hit nothing. The mattress bumped into Montoya's shins, then his knees before slamming back onto the ground and Montoya's feet.

Montoya stood, moisture from the mattress seeping into his shoes, and addressed the voice. "If you are the devil, leave this man's daughter be. In the name of Jesus Christ, get thee behind me, Satan."

A rush of air jetted by Montoya's ear. He felt more than heard the word *gladly* as a wind began to fill the room. The boards of the house shook as if rocked by an aftershock from the earlier earthquake. The front door slammed open, letting a shaft of light spill into the home. The boards settled; the room quieted. A fly buzzed somewhere in the house. No one said a word. A siren cried outside but faded to an echo before reaching the ears of the missionaries.

Faces peered in from the doorway, but the foul wind slammed the door again as it rushed back into the house and into the corner of the room where the men remained. A hand gripped Montoya's ankle and the voice spoke again, this time in Spanish.

"Aún no he terminado con ella…"

I'm not done with her yet.

Griffen lunged toward his companion and pulled the younger man away from the mattress. Fingernails ripped Montoya's trousers and stuck on his cotton socks before

Griffen was able to pull him out of the grasp of whatever lay upon the mattress.

"We need light and we need help," Griffen said to Montoya. He turned to the man who had brought them into this house and resumed his Spanish.

"We have to go get help," he told the man. "We will bring water, candles, and food."

"Traí a tu dios. Solo Él la puede salvar," the man replied.

"We will bring the Lord and all the angels of heaven to help your daughter," Montoya said as he wiped sweat from his brow. "We will bring Jesus."

"Jesucristo? Yes, bring your Christ and we will see who eats ash this day," the creature on the mattress said. The buzzing of the flies filled the space between words. "Bring Him to see me again."

Montoya turned away from the corner and investigated the man's face. "We will be back as soon as we can. I promise."

"Gracias, hermanos. Gracias. Gracias a Dios," he replied.

From behind the missionaries, the voice from the corner spoke again, but softer, sounding more like the daughter the man sought help for.

"Gracias élderes. Thank you, elders. Godspeed."

***

No words passed between Griffen and Montoya until they reached the home of their mission president, César Martínez. Griffen stopped Montoya just before the younger missionary could knock on the door.

"What do we say? What just happened back there?" Griffen said.

"We tell the truth. There was an earthquake. A man asked us to help his daughter. His daughter is sick with the devil." Montoya's matter of fact answer momentarily shocked

Griffen, but Griffen knew his companion was right. They would tell the truth.

President Martínez opened the door shrugging into his suit coat despite the increasing heat of the day. He took in the frightened faces and dusty shirts of the missionaries and Montoya's ripped pants in quick succession. He spoke Spanish, as is the general rule of the mission field to speak in the tongue as much as possible.

"Elders, you do not look so well," Martínez said. "Please come in."

"There was an earthquake, and someone needed help, and ..." Griffen started talking as fast as he could, but the last part stopped his voice.

"President, we need help. A man in the barrio says the devil has taken his daughter. Her hand ripped my pants, but I don't think it was truly her. We heard her speak in English and with a man's voice. The house is full of night and a terrible smell."

"Had you met this family before today?" Martínez said.

"No, president, we had not. We were in a home down the street giving Sister Molina a blessing," Griffen said. "Then there was the tremor and the man came looking for us to help."

Martínez glanced over both young men again, looking for any sign that they might be embellishing this story. He saw only fear and confusion on Elder Griffen's face. On Elder Montoya's, he saw fear and empathy.

"Take me there," Martínez said, grabbing the black-covered scriptures with his name embossed on the cover.

Griffen and Montoya had run so quickly from the barrio to Martínez's home that they did not notice how calm things were once they left the street they had been on. No signs of damage from the earthquake appeared despite the tremor occurring less than two hours before.

"President Martínez, did you feel the earthquake?"

Griffen asked.

"No, Elder, I did not. And there have been no reports of an earthquake on the radio."

"The earth reels to and fro like a drunkard. And shall be removed like a cottage," Montoya whispered.

"Yes, Elder," Martínez said. "Like tornadoes where I was raised in Oklahoma, an earthquake can hit one home or one street here. And they happen all too often. Your Book of Isaiah is strong."

The three men came to the street and were met by Brother Molina. He held the scriptures left behind by the elders and again gave his thanks to them and to God. But he could not bring gladness to his face.

"No vayan a aquella casa poh. Maricela ya no está bien poh y creemos que se enfermó hace rato ya," he said.

"Her name is Maricela? How long has she been sick?" Martínez asked.

"Desde que murió su madre. Juan, su padre, no está bien tampoco."

"The poor girl. So sick after losing her mother. Let us go see her and Juan," Martínez said.

The missionaries took their scriptures and shook hands with Brother Molina. If he had last warning, they did not see it. They did not look back as they scanned the buildings for Juan and Maricela's house. A path through some of the earthquake debris made walking down the street easier than it had been for Montoya and Griffen as they ran behind Juan earlier. Montoya was the first to spot the dark-cloaked figures keeping watch over the shack that held such horrible conditions inside.

Martínez walked up to the door but a hand shot out from the cloaks and grabbed him by the arm.

"Juan is dying. The devil has Maricela. You Mormon priests can't help them. Our Father will be here soon," said the figure that had reached out.

"We only want to do what we can," Martínez said. "Let us pass."

The arm retreated into the copse of black cloth and the Spanish litanies continued. Martínez, Griffen, and Montoya pushed open the door and plunged back into complete darkness.

The rattled boards seemed to fit better than when Montoya and Griffen had been inside the shack before; not even a shadow moved in the great room. Beyond the doorway into the second room, a rustling like rats running through an attic could be heard but not much else. As they moved closer to the door, Griffen tripped over what felt like a log. He reached down and grasped the hair on a cold leg.

"Juan," Griffen said, letting go of the leg. "We're back. We brought help."

Juan didn't answer. Instead, soft laughter began to replace the rustling from the second room.

"He's gone," said the gravel-tinged voice in English. "He has gone to see your Christ."

"We are all children of our Heavenly Father," Martínez said in Spanish. "Even you."

"Me?" The voice said. "Yo soy la hija del diablo."

The change to Spanish came with a return to the softer, more feminine voice.

Montoya stepped into the room and spoke louder than Griffen could remember hearing from his junior companion.

"Maricela, you are a daughter of the Lord and we are your brothers in Christ." Montoya reached into his pocket, grasping the plastic vial of consecrated oil and twisting the cap off with the same hand. "By the authority of the Melchizedek Priesthood which I hold, I anoint you with this oil in the name of Jesus Christ. Amen." He splashed the oil toward the mattress, following the groans to guide his hand, hoping enough of the oil reached Maricela to do any good.

Martínez and Griffen joined him and the three men

reached out to lay their hands upon Maricela together. A hand grabbed Martínez's coat and shoved him back. He regained his feet and scuffled back to the mattress.

Griffen yelped in pain as searing fingernails tore the skin off his left arm, but he didn't remove his hands from Maricela's body. Montoya dropped the empty vial and placed his hands next to Griffen's.

"Maricela," Martínez said, "by the authority of the Melchizedek Priesthood, which we hold, we bless you. Be healed from this attack. Be comforted in the knowledge that your Father in Heaven loves you. Be free from Satan's influence and forgiven of your sins in the name of Jesus Christ. Amen."

Griffen and Montoya echoed the *amen*.

The men left their hands on Maricela as her body thrashed on the soiled mattress. The stench around her worsened, then dissipated. She became still, her breathing shallow.

"We need to get a doctor for her and her father," Griffen said.

"We do," Martínez said. "But I fear this is just a moment of peace and not over."

Quietly, in her own voice and language, Maricela spoke. "He's not done with me yet."

"And we aren't, either," Montoya replied.

After some discussion and bringing another elder in to accompany him, Griffen headed out with Martínez's instructions.

Go back to the mission president's home, and speak to Sister Martínez.

Gather candles, water, and food.

Bring any of the other elders who might be around back to the barrio.

Make sure they have their scriptures.

Bring all the consecrated oil available. Get another bottle of olive oil to consecrate from Sister Martínez and ask her to call the doctor and give him directions to the home in the barrio.

Be back before the sun goes down.

Tell no man what has gone on today. Not Sister Martínez, not the doctor, not the other elders. They will learn soon enough.

With help from four other elders, Griffen packed enough food and water for two days. He deflected numerous inquiries before the scripture Martínez referenced came to him.

"Look it up," he told Elders Young, Draper, Lund, and Bracken. "Mark 7:36."

Griffen heard pages flipping behind him but he didn't stop. He adjusted the pack on his back and continued walking. Daylight was fading fast and he didn't want to come upon Maricela's house in the dark.

Griffen heard singing as he approached the home in the barrio. The dark-cloaked figures had moved on and in their place stood a tall man dressed in cotton pants and a loose-fitting, faded red shirt. The well-worn shirt was as wrinkled as his face. He held a small book in his hands and didn't look up as Griffen and the other elders approached the door.

"I am Maricela's uncle," he said in Spanish, keeping his eyes on his book. "Juan was my brother. Did the devil take my brother?"

"No," Griffen said as he pushed open the door. "Your brother is with Christ now, watching over his daughter."

"He died without a Priest to hear his final confession," the tall man said.

"Jesus heard him and that's what counts," Griffen answered, holding the door for the pack of white-shirted young men as they entered the shack. The door closed behind them. The tall man remained outside.

The singing Griffen had heard came from Martínez and Montoya. Someone had brought them a candle and the two men were sitting next to the mattress in the corner singing "I am a Child of God." Griffen set down his pack and joined them. The elders he brought with him did the same. The odor of the room felt less oppressive, as if pushed back by the range of male voices ringing out a song every Mormon child knew by heart.

As the verse ended and the candlelight wavered, Griffen glanced about for Juan but didn't see him. Tripping over the man's leg early and the appearance of his brother confirmed Griffen's fear that Juan was dead. President Martínez reached out to Griffen before the younger man could stand again.

"His brother came with some other men and they took Juan's body. They wanted to take Maricela, too, but she lashed out and struck one of them in the face. They don't know if he will still have vision in his left eye."

"The brother is still out there," Griffen said.

"And we are in here and will be until Christ Jesus releases this girl from her torment," Martínez said and began singing again.

In the waning candle's glow, Maricela's skin appeared green to Griffen. Her legs were bare up to mid-thigh. A shirt that might once have been white or yellow clung to her body as tightly as the drops of sweat on her brow.

"Siento sus ojos en mí, Virgen," said the softer voice to Griffen. "Toma lo que quieras."

"Do not listen, Elder Griffen," Montoya said as he put his hands on Griffen's shoulders. "It is not Maricela who speaks now."

Griffen nodded, wiped sweat off his forehead and gathered the four missionaries new to the scene to unpack the supplies they had brought. The men continued singing with their backs to Maricela as she enticed each of them to turn back to her and accept her invitation to join her on the mattress.

"Soy un hijo de Dios," they sang, reminding each other of their Father in Heaven. Their voices mixed with moans of bodily desire from the corner. Elder Draper, only in the field for three months, began to shake. He dropped a can of food on his foot, gasped, and cursed in the way only Mormons seem to do.

"Gosh darn it, that hurts," Draper said. He reached down and rubbed his foot through his shoe and stretched for the can he had dropped. He watched, bent over, as the can rolled to the mattress.

Broken-nailed fingers fondled the can, rolling it back and forth with fingertips still red from the blood of Montoya's leg and the eye of the man she struck. She seized the can in a crushing grip, shooting vegetable soup from both ends, some onto the mattress from one end and the floor on the other. The moans turned to laughter as the can momentarily disappeared. The eyes of all seven men in the room were now upon her, some wide with fear, others wanting to close but needing to see. Chunks of green and orange sludge dripped from the mattress and pooled on the floor. The candlelight flickered, revealing matted hair and blistered lips. Her head moved constantly, never letting the light touch her eyes.

The elders who had been stacking supplies joined Elder Montoya and President Martínez in a line by the mattress.

Elder Draper slipped in the small puddle of soup and fell to his hands and knees. As he looked up, the jagged edge of the tin can sliced into his throat. The disc of metal caught briefly against Draper's Adam's apple. Grunting, Maricela gripped the lid, letting it bite into the flesh of her palm, and pushed. The extra pressure forced the lid through the rest of Draper's throat, severing his vocal cords and windpipe. His hands flew to his neck, catching the lid in his right palm. Gouts of blood spurted from the slice in Draper's neck and from his pierced palm. Dark gore and bright oxygen-filled blood mixed and soaked his white shirt, flooding over his tie. Spurting blood splashed the shoes and pants of his brethren. A scream covered the raindrop sounds of blood spatter on leather shoes. Maricela's laughter dropped from inviting tones to a guttural, defiant timbre.

"You are all stained and can never be with your God now," the toad-like voice said in English. "Give yourselves to me and I will share this body with you."

Elder Young, who had been Draper's companion, raised his right fist to strike Maricela, but Montoya flung his arm out to block the strike.

"It is not her, Elder, who speaks, but if you hit her, it is her body that will feel it," Montoya said. "She will feel anything—anything—that happens to her body. Whatever has her wants you to hit her and more. We can't give in to this temptation."

Martínez moved out of line and put his hands on Young's shoulders. Young continued to stare down at Maricela.

"Montoya is right, Elder Young," Martínez said. "If any of us harm her, it will be as if we are prisoners on that same filthy mattress. We are not without sin, elders, so we shall cast no stones."

"Throw your stones, please," said the young woman. She spoke in her own voice, but in English. "Throw them and end this. Send me to Jesus." She stretched and writhed on the mattress, the skin on her thighs splitting as her legs shot out straight and pulled back against her body. Her tendons popped as if they were cooking and small streams of steam rose from the fissures in her flesh.

"¡Tráiganeme agua, tráiganeme agua!" Maricela spoke again in her own voice and language. Her arms flailed out above her prone body and the skin along her biceps tore, revealing the muscle beneath. More whitish jets of steam erupted from the canyons on Maricela's skin. The smell of burning flesh began to fill the room.

"What do we do?" Young asked Martínez, gripping his mission president's hands. "She's burning alive."

Martínez held Young's hands but turned to Montoya and then Griffen.

"What do we do?" Montoya said. Martínez gripped Young's hands harder and raised them for Montoya to see.

The other elders joined hands, Griffen and Montoya at each end. None of the men looked down at Elder Draper's body, now still, his tie almost invisible against his blood-darkened shirt.

Standing and now facing Maricela as her body burned from within, the men resumed their singing. Soon, Martínez began to pray again.

"Lord God, bless this day. Bless this day and take this woman's soul into your comfort," he prayed. He let go of the hands holding his and knelt before the mattress. Motioning the missionaries to join him, he placed his hands on Maricela's head. The other men placed their hands on her head, too, careful to avoid the pockets of fire oozing from her flesh. Montoya continued his prayer.

"O, Father, who art in heaven, bless this woman, Maricela. Help her to find peace in your bosom and rest at your throne. Peace may not be hers on earth, but it shall be her reward in heaven. Thou hast brought us here, humble before you, to confront evil. And after this day, we shall tell no man of it, as Thy scripture guides us to do.

"Thank you, O Lord, for Your son Jesus Christ, in whose name we pray today. Amen."

"Amen," the elders repeated.

"In the name of our Heavenly Father, we command that this woman be released. In the name of Jesus Christ, we pray. Amen," Montoya said.

Again, the young elders repeated their agreement. None lifted a hand away from Maricela as their palms blistered from the heat of her body. They pressed harder, each silently praying for her body and her soul.

Soon, the fire started to retreat from her flesh, the gashes melting back into smooth skin, and some of the men began to weaken and pull their hands back.

"This is not the end," Martínez whispered. He had felt the boiling subside as well, but took it more as a warning than a conclusion. He reapplied the pressure, the laying on of hands he so firmly believed in, and took a deep breath.

The warmth returned, but no to her body. Maricela's flesh cooled as the soiled mattress on which she lay caught fire. The flames spread up the wall, feeding on the brittle wood and disintegrating cardboard that held the shanty home together. The elders were forced to move back, but Martínez remained.

"This is not the end," he shouted. "By the power of our Heavenly Father; by the power of the holy Melchizedek Priesthood which we hold, we command you to release this woman and this home. We cast thee out, minion of Satan. Get thee behind us, devil!"

Elder Young wrapped his arms around his mission president and tried to pull him away, but the older man's body had become heavy and immobile. Elders Lund and Bracken went to them, each pulling Young from one side, but couldn't budge either man from where the knelt on the floor in front of growing flames.

"LEAVE THIS PLACE!" the croaking voice said, sending a gust of flames over the bodies of the four men nearest Maricela.

Montoya and Griffen, who had been the first to encounter this evil, stood by the door, watching as fire consumed the home, Maricela, and their mission brothers.

"LEAVE OR BE DEVOURED!"

The flames slithered across the floor and kissed the dark shoes of the two young elders. The door banged open and another burst of volcanic air forced them outside. They sat on the cold, dirt road and watched the walls collapse upon the six bodies inside, only one of whom was granted reprieve before the cleansing, consuming fire.

The flames didn't spread beyond the walls of the home but rather fed on everything inside. By the time the volunteer firefighters arrived, there was nothing left to be saved. Every sliver of wood, each chunk of flesh and bone that could be turned to ash had become so. Near the back of the lot, a pile of darkness rose slightly above the rest of the ash. As Montoya and Griffen stared at it, a breeze blew through and swirled the pile around, then left it indistinguishable from the rest of the cinders.

Montoya stood and pulled Griffen up with him. No one seemed to care who they were or why they were there. A small crowd had gathered and the two foreigners caught pieces of conversation in the language they were still learning.

¡Terromoto! ¡Terromoto! ¡El terromoto hizo el incendio!

And that was what they would believe and tell themselves for forty-five years: The earthquake caused the fire. Our friends were trapped inside. We were lucky to escape.

They would tell no man any different.

Chapter One: A Sunday

Brandon Smith only had to wake up early one day a week during the summer. Even on Saturdays, he could lounge in bed almost as long as he wanted, if he finished his chores before lunch. But Sundays? Up at six so he could get ready for church, help his brother David get ready for church, and then keep David out of Mom's hair so she could make breakfast and get ready for church.

He liked it better when his ward, Blackhawk Third Ward, started at eleven instead of nine. Sharing a building could be annoying—the time he left his Spider-Man notebook in the chapel and someone took it instead of turning it in to the lost and found box, for example—but getting to start late every other year helped.

Most of his friends from school were in the fourth ward, even though Bryce's family lived right behind the Smith home. Brandon didn't understand the strange ward boundaries and thought he might ask Bishop Griffen about it today. Even though he grew up Mormon, there was still a lot he didn't understand. His mind tried to map out what he thought the ward boundaries must be when the time to reflect ended.

"Brandon," his mom, Maddie, yelled from the kitchen. "Get up, now. David needs help with his socks before you take a shower."

Throwing off the quilt his grandma had made for him when he turned eight, Brandon stretched and yelled back. "He's nine, Mom, can't he put on his own socks?"

This was the wrong answer.

Before Mom could stomp to the top of the stairs, Brandon was out of his bed and with David in the living room, helping his brother pull thin black socks onto his feet, even though the younger Smith had only his underwear on. His church clothes sat lumped next to him, getting back some of the wrinkles Mom had so carefully ironed out yesterday.

"Hurry up, you two," Mom said, stopping at David's door. "We can't be late again. You're supposed to be passing the sacrament today, Brandon."

Remembering that, Brandon soon had David dressed, and had showered and dressed himself before meeting his mother and brother at the table. He devoured his breakfast before asking Mom for help with his tie.

"I can't get it right today," Brandon said. "The knot gets flipped around."

"You can wear mine," David said, offering his dark blue clip-on necktie to his brother.

"I'm a deacon now. I can't wear a clip-on. Mom, help," Brandon said.

Maddie knelt in front of Brandon, wrinkling her dress to match David's pants, and undid Brandon's red tie. She smoothed it out, lined up the pattern of white zig-zags, and knotted the tie around Brandon's neck in a flash.

"I used to have to straighten your dad's tie every Sunday," she said as she fixed Brandon's collar over his tie. "He could never get the knot right, either." She stood, ran her hands over the skirt of her dress, and turned away from her sons.

Brandon knew she was crying. He knew that at school, people still called her Mrs. Smith and Sister Smith or Sister Maddie at church. Here at home, she was still Mom. Here at home, Dad wasn't.

"Let's get in the car, boys," Mom said.

***

The deacons sat in the front row of the chapel. Brandon, the youngest of them, only got to pass the sacrament once a month since being ordained. Serving took eight deacons but there were fourteen deacons in the Third Ward, boys aged twelve and thirteen, so they had to trade around until some of the older boys turned fourteen and became teachers. Those boys would then prepare the bread and water used for the sacrament before the sacrament meeting began. At sixteen, they would move up and become priests. Priests, at least in the Church of Jesus Christ of Latter-Day Saints, blessed and officiated the sacrament and could do baptisms for new members. After that, when they were eighteen, they could go on a mission.

Brandon only occasionally thought of going on a mission. His father had served in Texas, before meeting Maddie, but it didn't seem to make him a better person. Besides, David would still need him around.

John Baxter, a thirteen-year-old, swatted Brandon with a program, bringing Brandon's mind back to the task at hand. "You ready?" John asked. "You can start at the front middle today. I'll do the bishopric and take the other side."

"Okay," Brandon said, opening his own program to see who would give the invocation—the opening prayer—and hoping it was someone who would keep it short. Brother Anderson, who lived down the block from the Smiths, was listed. Then Bishop Griffen would give the announcements. Then a hymn—Brandon's least favorite part of sacrament meeting because he couldn't sing well—and then they would bless and pass the sacrament.

The first parts ended quickly, and Brandon faked his way through one of the rotating sacramental hymns. Then he folded his arms and bowed his head, ready for the blessing of the bread.

One thing never confused Brandon: the sacrament prayers, the only prayers that were always the same. He'd read that other churches had bunches of prayers they repeated all the time. This made these prayers special, so special that, if a priest messes one up, he must start over. He listened as the priest asked for the blessing of God on the bread that is Christ's body. Standing with the other deacons, Brandon took his tray of bread and passed the first half of the sacrament. They lined up, returning the trays to the priests at the front of the chapel, and listened reverently through the prayer that blessed the water that is Christ's blood. Throughout both passes, the congregation barely made a sound. One man coughed, and a toddler dropped a baggie of Cheerios and asked her mom to get it.

Passing the sacrament became routine so quickly that Brandon hardly thought about it until he noticed his mom didn't take a piece of bread or the small cup of water when offered to her. He'd never known his mom to not take the sacrament. Even his little brother David, who had only been a real member since he turned eight and was baptized, took the sacrament. John nudged Brandon forward to return their water trays. The deacons and priests could then sit with their families.

Brandon sat next to his mom, too shocked to say anything to her even when she hugged him tight and whispered in his ear how proud of him she was.

The next two hours rushed by with Brandon replaying the image of his mother denying the sacrament. In the priesthood meeting, he remembered a talk about outer darkness, the place worse than Hell reserved for those with irrefutable proof of God and Jesus Christ who still denied them. Would his mom end up there, not even good enough for the terrestrial kingdom, let alone the celestial one where families would be together forever?

Here, surrounded by the men of his ward—the deacons, teachers, and priests of the Aaronic priesthood and the elders and high priests who held the Melchizedek priesthood—he wondered if anyone had reached the point of knowing God without a doubt. He heard it every week: they believed, they had faith, they knew without seeing. But had anyone he knew seen Heavenly Father and His son like they were taught Joseph Smith had?

Brandon glanced up and saw Bishop Griffen watching him. The bishop smiled and nodded his head toward Brother Jensen who had just reached the podium, and was ready to deliver a closing prayer. Brandon closed his eyes, bowed his head, folded his arms, and pondered outer darkness instead of listening to the prayer.

During Sunday School, Brandon managed to answer questions from Brother Atkinson, the deacons' teacher and former Boy Scout leader, about whether he would be at mutual on Wednesday. He wouldn't, he said, because he had to babysit David while his mom pulled the swing shift working cherries. Maybe next week.

On his way to the foyer, Brandon picked up David from his primary class. The two boys sat on a couch, waiting for their mom and some of the other Relief Society women to finishing gabbing about who needed a meal brought to them and what could be done for the Laughton family who lost a baby last month. As they waited, Bishop Griffen approached them and sat on the arm on the sofa.

"Good afternoon, Smith brothers," the bishop said. "How are you?" He extended his hand first to Brandon, then to David for the customary Mormon handshakes: always with the right hand, never with the left.

"We're good, Bishop," David said. "I think we're having roast again like last Sunday, but I think Mom might have forgot to make it."

"I'm sure she will have a fine Sunday dinner for her growing boys," Bishop Griffen said. "Brandon. How are you? I noticed you wool-gathering during the priesthood meeting. The Lord is our shepherd, you know, so I hope you were only thinking of helping Him out."

"I'm sorry I wasn't paying attention in the meeting. Just some stuff on my mind," Brandon said.

"Do you want to talk about it? We need to talk soon, anyway, before the next temple trip to do baptisms for the dead."

Some of Brandon's concerns lifted from his shoulders at the thought of going to the temple. He had sung about how he loved to see the temple since he was in primary. His favorite temple was the one in Manti, a couple hours south of Blackhawk. His grandparents had been married there and the Mormon Miracle Pageant was held there every summer. But he wouldn't be going there to do baptisms for the dead. He and the other young men and women from the Blackhawk Third Ward would go to the new Blackhawk Temple that opened the previous fall. First, though, he would need to meet with Bishop Griffen to receive his temple recommend.

"Mom's working cherries, swing shift, this week."

"How about next Tuesday morning, then? Ten o'clock? You won't even have to wake up early."

Maddie Smith joined them then and smiled.

"My boy getting a meeting about a recommend? Bishop, Ill be sure hes on time," Maddie said.

The bishop shook hands with them and even pulled a mint out of his pocket for David. "I will see you next Sunday and the Tuesday following, Brother Smith."

***

No Sunday roast awaited the Smith boys at home. Brandon had washed the roasting pan himself after last week's dinner, so he knew there must be another reason why his mom hadn't made a roast like she did almost every

Sunday. Chicken and ground beef sat in the freezer, solid as ice. A frozen pizza, a stack of pot pies and a box of corn dogs from last year took up the bulk of the freezer space.

"What's for dinner, Mom?" Brandon shouted, not knowing where Maddie was. David came into the kitchen and mouthed the word *roast*. Brandon shook his head and called out again. "Mom?"

The boys waited quietly for their mom to at least acknowledge them. After a long silence, Brandon spoke.

"You stay here. Mom might have gone outside to water her flowers."

"But that's working on the Sabbath!" David said.

"It's all right. You can do stuff to keep your plants and animals alive. You just wait here."

Brandon didn't make it to the front door. As he walked through the house, he could hear his mom crying and talking to someone on the phone in her bedroom. The door was opened enough for him to see her sitting on her bed, one hand holding the phone to her ear and the other covering her eyes.

"Yes, thank you," she said into the phone through a heavy sigh. "They can play. Brandon won't mind watching David for a few extra minutes. Goodbye, Bishop."

Brandon knocked on the door and peeked his head inside. "Mom, are you okay? David is wondering what's for dinner."

"Oh, honey. Mom just needs a rest. I know we were saving that pizza, but if you want to make it, you can. You won't even have to save me a slice. I'm just going to lay here for a while, okay? Come get me after you eat."

Kids learn to cook from their parents. Brandon did not pre-heat the oven. He placed the frozen pizza on the bottom side of a turned over cookie sheet. He gathered the small bits of cheese that fell off and one stray pepperoni slice and put them back on the pizza. In 15-18 minutes, the Smith boys would have an entire pizza to themselves, which had never happened. They were also going to watch TV on a Sunday afternoon, another rarity.

The cable left when Dad left, limiting their options. During the fall, David liked to watch football when Mom allowed, but Brandon preferred baseball or movies. All four channels had infomercials running, so they'd have to watch a movie instead. Mom kept the slim selection of R-rated movies in her room, along with most of the PG-13 ones. What remained was a stack of seemingly ancient Disney cartoons in their plastic clamshell cases, LDS comedies on DVD like "The RM," and the James Bond 007 movies Dad didn't take with him.

"Can we watch 'Hercules,' please," David asked.

"Yep," Brandon said, grabbing the fat VHS case and putting the tape into one side of their double machine. He hit play, then went back to the kitchen to wait for the pizza to be done. The previews and opening credits ended at about the same time Brandon returned to the living room with two plates loaded with pizza. He set them down, went back to the kitchen, and returned with two tall, cold glasses of Sprite.

Since the movie continued well after the Smith boys had finished their pizza and each had had a second glass of Sprite, Brandon decided to let Maddie sleep until the end of the show. She needed the rest, he knew, especially before her new shift at the cherry plant started. She had been on the graveyard shift at first, but last week she'd told Brandon they were paying a bonus to anyone who'd work swings in order to get more workers on that shift. "We need the money," shed said. "And it's only until school starts up again." It meant Brandon would miss most of the Young Men's activities and the monthly Mutual meeting where the young men and the young women joined together. Like all the young men he knew, Brandon was fascinated by the young women he knew.

He also knew that if he thought about them too much, he'd have to tell Bishop Griffen about it.

So he let his mom sleep until the end of the movie. And he let her sleep through David's bath time. He let her sleep as he put himself to bed.

Brandon even let her sleep after he awoke from a nightmare in which she, his precious mother, floated in outer darkness, forever separated from her family and from Heavenly Father. She floated through a city he didn't recognize, but he could see a temple being built in the distance, the tall, white spire reaching toward heaven, but the Angel Moroni not yet in place atop it. Then she fell into a fire that engulfed the city. Before she could call for help, Brandon awoke.

Chapter Two: Monday

Maddie woke, still in her Sunday dress, groggy and unsure of the time. The right side of her face peeled away from the blankets, sticky with drool and sweat, as she lifted her head to look at the clock. The red numerals taunted her, **2:15** with the small dot indicating *p.m.* missing, meaning the summer sunrise wouldn't come for another two and a half hours. The boys wouldn't be up until well after that. She had planned to practice her new hours Sunday night, but the day overwhelmed her. The heat, watching her son pass the sacrament, then hearing him arrange a meeting with the bishop... it all got to her in unexpected ways.

But none of them were the entire truth of why she had slept the Sunday away after making her own appointment with Bishop Griffen. Two pieces of paper sat on her dresser, unseen from her position on the bed, but never out of her mind. The first, a yellow carbon paper indicating her shift change at the cherry plant wasn't that bad. The lie shed told Brandon about it, though, weighed on her. Yes, she would get a small raise, but it was a tiny reward for being moved away from a shift supervisor who was more interested in kissing her during lunch break than in doing his job.

The second piece of paper—white with large red letters stamped across it—noted her defeat. The lowing-paying summer jobs she'd held over the last two years, the eternal struggle of a teacher's salary in Utah, and the lack of a child support payment over the second half of that time combined into one of the worst words she had ever read: **FORECLOSURE**.

She was supposed to be able to raise her sons in this house, in her hometown, with her husband, but soon the house would belong to the bank just as her husband now belonged to someone else. She would talk to Bishop Griffen about it next Tuesday. Until then, she still had to make it through this Monday.

Making breakfast for her sons would be a good start. She could sleep a few more hours and then face the day with her brave boys. Maddie slipped off her dress and pantyhose, and pulled a nightshirt over her head before unhooking her bra and letting it drop to the floor. She lay back down, the nightshirt flush against her body, and stayed on her side of the bed despite two years of having the whole queen-sized bed to herself.

When sleep came again, the dark still held off the sun and there were no dreams.

***

Like all the days Maddie had known before, the sun rose and the Lord had not yet come again. She thanked Heavenly Father and Jesus for Brandon's ability to pour himself and his little brother cereal, even though she wished they'd pick something else besides marshmallow-loaded sugary cereals. At least they didn't mind the ones in the big bags and names just a bit off from the major brands.

She could hear them downstairs, gobbling their breakfast and watching TV. She could leave them like that all day and they would be fine. Hiding in her bedroom, avoiding the tasks ahead of her over the next few days: these were not the worst ideas she'd ever had. Letting Everett Slocumb kiss her once had been the worst idea she'd had recently. He wanted another kiss the next day and more than that soon enough. Luck—or God's grace as she would likely be reminded during her meeting with the bishop—was on her side. Maddie Smith was not the first woman Everett had set his sights on. Instead of getting fired or flat out suing Everett and the whole cherry-picking company, Maddie took the swing shift and the $1.50 raise that came with it. Sometimes, *You have to take the easy way out, even if it's not the best way*, Maddie thought.

Tears threatened to consume her again. Her husband, her ex-husband, the jerk, said something similar during their divorce. Easier for him to ride away on his motorcycle than try to make their marriage work. Easier to party with twenty-somethings than to play catch with his sons. *Jackass*, she thought. It was the level of swearing she used most, and that made her want to cry more. Maddie didn't need to cry now. What she needed was a shower and a bowl of rainbow-colored cereal. She'd take the sugar rush now and hope it lasted her until lunch, when she would allow herself a Diet Coke. She'd long ago accepted caffeine into her life, but still couldn't come to grips with the smell of coffee. Yes, a Diet Coke and a nice tomato sandwich after her morning appointment.

But first, a shower.

Brandon and David were still watching TV as Maddie walked into the living room. The shower refreshed her, but it would still be a long day.

"Hey, guys," she said, standing in front of the TV. "Listen up for a minute."

Brandon stopped the tape they were watching and nudged David into an upright position. "What's up?"

"I gotta go out for a bit. I know that means you'll be stuck with each other even longer today since I have to work earlier, but I promise I'll make it up to you."

"Can we go, please?" David said.

"No, buddy, but if I can, I'll bring you a treat."

"Cheeseburgers?" David asked.

"Not today, but we can maybe go to Walt's this week. But only if Brandon tells me you've been good."

"I'll be good," David said.

"Brandon, you still with us?" Maddie said as she noticed her oldest son's attention drifting.

"Yeah, I'm here. We'll be fine," Brandon said.

Maddie didn't care for the teen-like sullen tone in Brandon's voice. Scolding him now, however, would make the chances of a fight-free day slim to none. "Thank you, Brandon. I owe you one."

She walked out the door, turning to wave goodbye one more time before closing it behind her. Brandon waved back, leaving her wondering why he didn't ask her where she was going.

"Turn the show back on, Brandon," David said.

***

The three-bedroom, two-bathroom house on 600 North sat clustered by walnut trees on a corner like every other corner in Blackhawk. Summer toys lay scattered across the lawns of the neighboring homes. The smell of tar from the annual chip sealing wafted on the air, reminding Maddie of her childhood when she and her cousins told each other it was so hot the road was melting. A black and orange **FOR RENT** sign had been stapled to a tree near the street. The orange letters were going white, faded from not just this summer but the last two, as far as Maddie knew. The phone number on the sign still worked, and the rental price, with sewer, water, and garbage paid, cut her housing expenses almost in half.

"No one's been murdered in there or anything like that," the property manager had told her on the phone. "Legally, I have to tell you if someone had. I just can't keep anyone in the house for very long. The owner got sick of trying to sell it. No one has even called about it since last summer."

Being desperate, Maddie agreed to look at it. She'd picked up a set of keys from the property manager before driving to the house. She hadn't had to look at a house or apartment in so long that she didn't think much of it when the manager told her she could take the keys as long as she brought them back before the office closed at 4:30.

Maddie stood on the porch. The white paint was peeling off the concrete columns and wooden overhang. She felt ... nothing. She had expected another burst of tears at the thought of losing her house, her home, but didn't feel the sadness that had plagued her daily since her divorce. She didn't feel the joy that some experience when seeing their dream homes for the first time. She didn't feel the trepidation that seemed to ooze off the property manager. Another wave of nothingness ran over Maddie as she turned the key and pushed open the front door. The weight of emptiness rushed across her shoulders and through her legs. A deep, interior darkness swelled inside her as her feet crossed the threshold. A breeze from outside fluttered a curtain in the front room and the darkness broke for a moment. Maddie's feet carried her deeper into the house, small pockets of sunlight showing her the way to lamps the property manager said would work. Once the lights had been turned on, the house no longer seemed full of darkness. Instead, it was full of dust. Strips of ancient wallpaper mixed with plaster fallen from the walls and ceiling littered the floor. She stepped on a piece of lathing, splintering the piece of wood and the silence surrounding her.

Wings fluttered somewhere above her and small, clawed feet skittered around her although she saw neither bird nor rat. The grit of the room—plaster, disintegrating wood, dander of countless animal squatters—tickled her face with unpleasant, invisible fingers. Maddie stepped into the touch and through it, deeper into the house. To the right, a study; ahead the kitchen. Between those rooms and down a short hall were stairs to the second level. Through the kitchen were stairs to a cellar.

Maddie took the stairs up, each creaking away the years since they'd last been trod upon. With every step up, the beating of wings lessened. Maddie hoped any birds there would be gone before she summited the steps. The landing loomed above her, stretching toward the apex of the house. She stopped two steps from the top and stared down a hallway. Two closed doors on the right, one on the left. A third door at the end of the hall stood slightly ajar.

Maddie took another step toward the second floor and the door at the end of the hallway opened another inch. She mounted the final step and the opening widened again. By the time Maddie was on the same level and in the hallway, the door gaped halfway open, inviting Maddie to come on in, look around, stay for a while.

"The second floor has a master bedroom, two smaller bedrooms, and a linen closet," the real estate agent had said. "The master is truly remarkable."

Maddie reached out and tapped the door to open it fully. She expected sunlight to hit her face. There was light, but it wasn't the sun. A deep red assaulted her, diffuse but potent. Unlike the barrenness of the rest of the house, thick carpet blanketed the floor of the master bedroom. Tapestry-like curtains hung over the windows, preventing any illumination from outside. Maddie reached for a light switch but pulled her hand back upon touching the wall. She stepped deeper into the room and turned toward the wall.

Stretching her hand out again, Maddie caressed the velvety wallpaper. A crimson glow pulsed off the walls, providing the strange light shed seen upon entering the room. How wallpaper could glow was beyond Maddie. Touching it, however, thrilled her and gave her a sense of revulsion like biting into a peach just beyond ripe. The fuzziness tickled her fingertips but if she lingered in one spot too long, the wall began to feel alive. It writhed beneath her fingers as she moved around, dragging her hand along the wall. Thrilling and disgusting, reviling and arousing. She continued around the room, not yet wanting to disengage from the sensations of the wall.

At the farthest point from the door, Maddie placed both hands on the wall. The fine hairs on her arms and at the back of her neck stood up. The hairless undersides of her arms felt as though a million tiny feet, all wearing cotton-soft baby booties, were walking to her shoulders. Once there, the feeling solidified, became a hand on each shoulder, pushing out the tension that had built inside her. The sensation spread, the feet traipsing down her body, over her breasts, across her abdomen, along her hips, and—oh! between her legs. But as the rest of her body felt the invisible assault, Maddie noticed the sensation of hands remained on her shoulders. As she took note of the hands again, trying to ignore the filthy and pleasant tingling at her most private place, they tightened. The grip of whatever held her strengthened.

When the hands started to move to her neck, Maddie pushed herself away from the wall.

"Lord," she said. "Lord, what is in here?"

The tingling, the pressure, the grip, lifted away from her immediately. She stared at the wall, the dust in front of her eyes making it appear as if the wall had wrinkled. She watched something beneath the wallpaper slither to the floorboards and stifled a scream. In her next breath, she sucked in the dust and began to choke.

Rushing out of the room and into the kitchen, she prayed that the water would be on. Maddie wiped tears and a silty layer of dust from her face with one hand as the other lifted the handle on the ancient faucet. The water came on, and Maddie filled her cupped palm with it. Her eyes flew open at the taste of the water: ash. And when she saw the blood-red pool of liquid in her hand, the scream shed held back moments before escaped. She felt the atmosphere around her pulling at her breath, as if it lived on the sound of her terror.

She gagged and spat, trying to get the burnt flavor off her tongue. Slowly, her breathing returned to normal, her vision cleared, and she knew she had to leave the house. There would be other rentals. She'd find somewhere for her children to live and be safe, somewhere where she could protect them from…from what?

From everything.

As she gathered herself, the creaking of an opening door reached her ears. She looked around and saw the door to the basement had opened. A soft yellow light glowed from beyond the door, much more inviting than the scarlet tones of the room upstairs. She promised the real estate agent she would give this house a fair shake and, unlike her husband, she kept her promises. Nothing here could hurt her as long she watched her step.

The top stair did not make a sound and held her wobbling legs like a sturdy foundation. Each step down gave her more confidence, until she touched the dirt floor and the door above her slammed shut.

Standing still, Maddie felt her feet sink into the dirt floor even though her shoes didn't leave the dusty surface. The pull from below pinned her to the spot at the base of the stairs and she couldn't turn around to see if the door had closed or if it was just her imagination. Some strange gravity pulled the door shut, held her in place, and tried to wrench another scream out of her. Her imagination screamed, telling her something would creep up behind her, grab her around the throat like the presence in the master bedroom, and never let her out of the house.

Brandon and David would be lost. Lost boys with no Peter Pan to guide them to Neverland. She had to get home. She had to take a step, turn around and get out.

The glow that enticed her down the stairs shimmered and grew, filling her eyes until she had to squint against it just to keep her thoughts steady. She lifted a foot and planted it back down on the dirt floor, hoping she had turned and was headed toward the stairs. One more step and she should feel the bottom rung. She slid her other foot forward, searching for the step but only putting more dirt into the bright air. She took another step and slide, this time with her hands in front of her, but still didn't connect with the wooden steps that would grant her escape. She stretched her sliding foot another few inches, shuffled the other foot to catch up and repeated the motion. She stumbled forward when her leading foot hit something solid, but not far. Her foot had reached the outer wall of the basement and her hands landed on what felt like a window ledge.

Opening her eyes, Maddie discovered the light had shut off. Behind her, her tracks—one solid line next to a set of prints from a single foot, then short gliding prints with small mounds of dirt—never faced the stairs. The door above remained shut, a thin line of light peeking under it. She swung her head back to the front and saw that her hands were not on a window as she had hoped but rather on a thickly-framed piece of art. Her fingers scraped against the canvas, and the sensation of something living beneath her fingertips that shed felt in the master bedroom returned.

The dark wood of the frame made her think of antiques, of things her boys would grow bored of seeing on museum field trips. The sturdiness made her think of the chapel of her wardhouse and the pews filling it, as well as the podium from which members of the congregation gave their talks while the bishopric sat nearby, usually attentive, sometimes as sleepy as the members staring back at them.

Maddie then thought of sleep and how nice it would be to lay down on the cold dirt floor and dream her ruined life away.

The tickling at her fingertips roused her and she opened her eyes wider to take in the painting held in place by the heavy frame. Maddie wished she hadn't looked.

Before her lived a scene her mother would have used to scare her when she was a child, if her mother had had any imagination. Utah hadn't escaped the "satanic panic" of the 1980s, and Maddie still remembered hearing bits and pieces about devil worshipers in the canyons and cults of Mormons who fell away soon after the pioneers settled in Salt Lake. This painting somehow survived that era when her mother's warning was simply to stay away from the kids who only wore black all the time.

The painting showed a clearing in a forest. A young woman, stripped to the waist, kneeled in what looked like prayer in the middle of the clearing. Three men, nude from the waist down and aroused, stood behind the woman to one side. In front of her, also nude and aroused, stood the devil as Maddie knew him: red-skinned with huge horns growing from his forehead and the feet of a goat. The devil's rigid member nearly touched the kneeling woman's forehead and his black beard grew to touch the top of her head. The work was clearly that of an amateur, but one with promise. Maddie took her eyes away from the primary scene of the painting and noticed a house in the background, windows lit through the trees.

The house in the painting was the house she was in.

As she stared into the painted windows, her right hand moved up the painting and caressed the canvas between the praying woman's face and the tip of the devil's penis. The lights of the painted house flickered, and Maddie's vision briefly went dark. She saw herself as the woman, the three men behind her laughing, the devil grunting with anticipation. The image lasted but a moment only to be replaced by another: her body, dead, buried beneath the dirt of the basement floor she stood on.

Maddie screamed and pulled her hands away from the painting, found the stairs with her eyes, and rushed up them, through the house, and into the fresh air outside. She didn't see the skinless finger, just one bleached-bone tip, that the dirt she kicked up in her haste uncovered.

Chapter Three: Tuesday

Cameron ordered the fish and chips for his grandma, who had lived in the foothills of the Wasatch mountains since her twenties. Grandpa used to get them for her every year for her birthday. Cameron continued the tradition years after both passed away and sometimes even on days other than Grandma's birthday.

The deluxe bacon double cheeseburger was his. The crisp bacon and two patties with American cheese melting between them battled the acidic bite of the tomato slice and went best with onion rings rather than fries.

He ordered fries, too, to dip in his mother's chocolate malt, just like she did when he was a kid. One fry at a time, deep into the thick, cold malt. Walt's still made their own fries: potatoes trucked south from Idaho, fresh-cut in the restaurant, served hot with the oil still dripping off them. If he wasn't having the malt, Cameron would use Walt's homemade fry sauce. Then again, he might still need the tangy pink dip for the onion rings and English chips.

Walt—and somehow decades of employees—kept the recipe for the fry sauce a secret even though everyone knew it was just ketchup and Miracle Whip instead of mayonnaise, no relish. The secret recipe remained popular years after Walt had died and even after his small-town burger joint in the heart of Blackhawk, Utah, took on a different name. Walt's would always be Walt's to the older generations of Blackhawk residents and to those like Cameron who had lived his whole life—all forty years of it—there. Cameron claimed a history with Blackhawk older than the first McDonald's in town and so when he needed to eat, which he did more often than the average person, he ate at Walt's.

Sometimes he ate at Two Hawks Pizza on the edge of downtown, even though it was more expensive than a chain pizzeria and the dough didn't always cook right. The pizzas always seemed to have an oily taste to them, like the ovens were fueled by the mechanic's shop next door, but they loaded each pie with toppings and never looked at Cameron funny when he also ordered cheese bread with his large combination pizza.

For a few years, he'd eaten dinner at this place where you'd call your order in from a phone at your table, then pick it up and pay at the counter. He would sit in a corner where the cook couldn't see him so when he ordered a Philly cheesesteak, a shrimp basket, and mozzarella sticks, it wouldn't seem weird. On the night before the place closed, Cameron ordered three sets of their most expensive meal: 10-ounce ribeye with a baked potato smothered in butter, sour cream, ranch dressing, cheese, and chives. He cleaned each plate and left a tip he couldn't afford.

He was single and tipped better than most individual diners when he could, but he hardly ever went to restaurants that had servers and required tipping. They weren't so kind when he ordered more than one entrée. They didn't know he was eating for his whole family.

He didn't need to tip at the Daley Freez, his preferred late-afternoon dessert and soda stop on the other side of Blackhawk from Walt's. They made soft serve ice cream cones so tall that Cameron couldn't drive and eat one at the same time. Their vanilla always had a slight pineapple taste to it that he learned to love as kid. Daley Freez always put a small plastic circus animal toy on top of each cone back then. They hadn't done that in years, or maybe they did but just for kids. Cameron didn't have kids. His family was still in town, though, next to each other in a nice row with a well-maintained lawn.

His lunch order—the food he ordered for his family, he reminded himself—filled two trays. The high school girls behind the counter never said a word about what he ordered, or his almost three-hundred-pound, five-and-a-half-foot tall body, in front of him and if they talked when he wasn't there, he didn't care. He needed to eat; he would eat at Walt's even if they called the place the Heart Attack Zone or Drive-in Diabetes. He would eat at Walt's until he couldn't fit in the booth, which, really, wasn't that far ahead in his future.

He scarfed his meals in record time that June Tuesday. Usually, at that point, Cameron knew he had had enough. He'd even slurped down his huge root beer before the crushed ice melted. He fished half a French fry from the dregs of his chocolate malt and wondered if he should order a sundae. They used those candied cherries he'd hated since childhood, but he could make an exception today just to get more of the real whipped cream he loved. He took his empty trays up to the counter and waited until one of the girls saw him.

"You know you don't have to bus your table, Mr. Eckhart," said the redhead behind the counter. "What else are we supposed to do on slow days?"

"Thanks, Amber, but I'd like to place another order."

"What are you having?"

Cameron told her and said he'd have his order to stay.

About ten minutes later, Amber brought him his hot fudge sundae, with the dreaded maraschino cherry sinking into the fresh cream, a chicken cordon bleu sandwich, a steak salad with extra tomatoes and onions, a refill on his extra-large root beer, another order of onion rings, and two dishes of fry sauce.

"You let me know if you need me to bag any of that up," Amber said, brushing stray bun crumbs off her silver and green Blackhawk High T-shirt. "I'd eat the sundae first. It's about 200 degrees outside."

Cameron nodded, his mouth already stuffed with an onion ring. A dollop of fry sauce escaped his lips as he nodded. He followed the wayward pink goo's trajectory and watched it splatter as it hit his black sweat pants. The pink immediately darkened, but Cameron didn't lift his head again. Beneath his table, he saw a small creature. At first he thought that it might be a raccoon because everything around its eyes appeared black. Then he noticed the complete lack of color beyond the eyes. He could just make out a form from which the eyes peered, yet all else was cloaked in darkness. The thing's body squirmed in the pitch black like a cat beneath a quilt. The eyes, stark white in the shadows, stared at Cameron and Cameron could do nothing else but stare back.

When Cameron began to wonder if he would ever be released from the creature's gaze, a sliver of red appeared below the eyes. A mouth Cameron feared would be full of razor-sharp teeth opened. To his relief, there seemed to be no teeth at all. Instead, a tongue the color of the cherry Cameron had allowed to taint his sundae lolled out of the mouth and reached up to lick the spatter of fry sauce from Cameron's pants. The thick tongue lingered on Cameron's thigh and he could feel its taste buds searching for more sustenance through the cotton covering his leg.

With his head still down, Cameron tried to muster a scream, even it if meant embarrassing himself in front of the crew and other customers. He knew in his heart that Amber would tell her friends behind the counter—and continue telling others when school started—that the fat guy who always ordered like he was feeding a family of four freaked out in the restaurant. Mrs. Smith, a grade-school teacher

Cameron saw at church every Sunday and on the days he substituted on the elementary janitorial crew, sat two booths away with her sons. She would tell all his former teachers and Bishop Griffen that he had screamed like a girl at something under the table that was probably just a wad of old gum, melting in the heat and dripping onto his thigh.

The thing beneath the table held his sight until Cameron felt rough scratching on his calf. He looked up as the creature's claws tore through his sweats and burrowed into his flesh. Then he felt more pressure against his shin as the thing pulled itself against Cameron and began to crawl up his leg, using its claws and tongue—now wrapped completely around Cameron's trunk-like thigh—to hoist itself from below.

As the mutant clawed up his leg, Cameron panned around Walt's to see if anyone could help. He heard Amber and the rest of the staff giggling somewhere out of sight. He looked across the restaurant, hoping Mrs. Smith was still there, or one of her boys, the oldest who could perhaps help Cameron remove the creature from his leg.

He saw neither of the Smith boys. Walt's had begun to take on the same shadowy hue as the space beneath Cameron's table. The darkness, however, wasn't spreading from his booth but rather from the table Mrs. Smith occupied. She looked at Cameron and the black surrounded her just as it had the creature before. Soon Cameron could only see her eyes shining white in the darkness ... and her mouth, which hung open so low that Cameron couldn't see her bottom jaw. The lower half of her face pulsed first with an inky darkness and then with a fleshy cherry-red that slithered down her body and beneath the tabletop in front of her. Cameron looked into the transparent pits of her eye sockets and the shadows drooped for a moment, as if to wink at him. She lifted her head and he felt the creature on his leg tug back just a bit at the same time Mrs. Smith's mutated tongue seemed to pull back into her mouth. The tongue around his thigh then loosened for a split second before reaffirming its grip as Mrs. Smith lowered her head again.

With two sets of the same alien, white eyes upon him, Cameron tried to slide out of the booth, but the demon—Mrs. Smith, he admitted to himself, although he didn't understand—jolted backward and forced him to his rear. He slid the other way, smashing his shoulder into the plate-glass window of Walt's.

Cameron looked out the window but saw only more of the moist velvet darkness through it. No cars on the old highway, no gas station across the street, no discount pizza parlor next door.

Night had fallen over Blackhawk during lunch hour.

Closing his eyes made no difference. Cameron could see only the cherry red of the tongue that grew from Mrs. Smith's head and became the tongue of a clawed beast, and the stark whiteness of four eyes, all staring at him, drilling this madness into his head.

The creature, simultaneously a monster and a school teacher, wrenched Cameron downward, forcing him beneath the table. The tongue-beast flexed, pulling and squeezing him through the legs of the tables and booth seats. As he slid along the floor, mopping up all manner of goop from under him and sticking to even more from the other tables above him, Cameron had one final thought.

I think I've lost my appetite. It's ruined.

The mutant Mrs. Smith swallowed Cameron, using the tongue-beast to propel him down her gullet, stopping only once to widen her mouth around his enormous gut. Once her mouth had closed, the light returned to Walt's and to Blackhawk.

"Mr. Eckhart didn't finish his rings," Amber said, now two tables away from where Cameron had been devoured. "Did you see him leave, Mrs. Smith?"

"No, I didn't," Mrs. Smith said. "How shameful of him to waste food."

"Yeah, not like him at all, but at least he paid for it," Amber said as she began clearing the table.

"He certainly did," said Mrs. Smith, licking a dab of fry sauce from her lips.

***

The clock flashed midnight when Maddie awoke from the second nightmare, the one in which she saw herself consume innocent Cameron Eckhart, one of the janitors from school. But it couldn't be midnight. She'd come home from touring that wretched house, showered, slept through the afternoon and then went to work at the cherry plant. It could not be midnight because she had been watching the oversized digital clock ticking away the minutes until her shift ended as Monday turned into Tuesday. She stretched on her bed, the odd nightmare fading away faster than the one she'd had before it. She'd have to tell someone about the first dream; the second—and similar dreams of devouring people she knew—could swirl down the memory toilet for all she cared.

She opened her bedroom door and immediately heard the chaos.

"Mom's up and I'm going to tell!" David shrieked the way only younger brothers tattling on older brothers can.

"You'd better not. I got it fixed," Brandon said.

"Fixed what, guys?" Maddie asked, interrupting the exchange between her sons.

"Nothing," Brandon said. "The power went out and I fixed it."

"He touched the box, Mom. The one you said to never touch," David said.

"Honey, you're right. You aren't supposed to touch that. But sometimes, we must do things that aren't quite right in order to get other things right, like getting the electricity back on." David looked dejected, but Brandon didn't take the chance to gloat like many kids his age would have. Maddie found a smile for them both. "Now, why don't you tell me what time it is so I can fix my clock."

"It's ten o'clock and all is well," David sang out.

"Good. Did you guys plan lunch yet? Maybe we can go to Wa…" Maddie's sentence faded as bits of her dream came back to her: a man she knew stuffing his face at Blackhawk's favorite greasy spoon, her shoving his body down her throat as he screamed.

"Mom? Are you okay?" Brandon said. "You look like you swallowed a bug."

"I'm fine, just lost my train of thought. Let's go to Walmart, I was going to say, and get hoagie fixings."

***

The hoagies hit the spot for everyone. Maddie splurged and let the boys pick brand-name sodas instead of the store brand and they each got to choose a bag of chips to go with the sandwiches. Instead of going home to eat, they went to Memorial Park and sat beneath the trees that were planted a century before to honor soldiers from Blackhawk who died during World War I. Somewhere, Maddie had a book with a map that marked which tree was planted for each soldier. The park also gave her the chance to be outside instead of in the house that was being taken from her, or the cherry plant that steadily filled with the odors of steam and sour cherries. And, mostly, outside and away from any upstairs rooms with living walls and dirt-floored basements with paintings of Lucifer.

Brandon and David jostled each other, punching an arm here and tousling hair there, as Maddie's mind and eyes wandered. She took in the blue sky and the wisps of clouds. She saw the trees and the grass, the white bandstand that still hosted a community band on summer Sunday nights. She noticed a few people, unsupervised children playing with kids whose mothers stood scant yards away, a smattering of elderly folks dressed like her parents would be if they'd been alive, a twenty-something couple gazing into each other's eyes, and a trio of men who seemed to be staring at her.

The men were not dressed in black shirts, but at least they were dressed. Maddie couldn't remember if their faces were uncovered the last time she saw them, but she knew these were the men from the painting, although they looked older. She stared back, whispering a prayer to herself. The lips of the men moved, too, until one by one, they each placed a single finger in front of their lips. Maddie looked away to see if anyone else saw the trio, but they were gone when she turned back.

**

On the phone, behind her locked door, Maddie wanted to tell her best friend Heather everything. Heather always listened and had been listening to Maddie since junior high. Maddie wanted to tell her about the nightmares. The dream about Cameron would scare Heather, but it would only make sense if Maddie told her about the dream she had before that one. And that would only be clear if Maddie revealed the foreclosure notice and her trip to the sandstone house.

"Okay," Heather said, talking on what was undoubtedly a recently released smartphone and coming through to Maddie's landline. "That all sounds horrible. Now tell me what's really bothering you."

"I dreamt I was the woman in the painting," Maddie said. "Oh, gosh, it was so gross. That... that thing... was in my face and I couldn't get away. But in the dream, part of me didn't want to. I haven't been with anyone since Alex left and, I wasn't with anyone before. But I wanted it, *him*, so bad that it hurt."

"The bishop wouldn't approve, but you need to get some action or take care of it yourself," Heather said, giggling as if they were talking about cute boys in their sophomore biology class.

"It's not funny. There's more. In the dream, when *he* was done, those other men took me into the house and threw me into the basement. I woke up when I hit the dirt floor. And I know it can't be—I couldn't see their faces in the painting—but the men I saw in the park were them."

"Oh, Maddie. You're right. That can't be because it was a dream and half-naked men don't walk out of a painting in some old creepy house. You should…wait, hang on. I have another call."

Maddie heard a click and expected hold music, like from a customer service line. At first there was only silence. The silence soon seemed to become a pulse, and then a breath, to Maddie. Then she thought she heard a voice.

"Heather, are you there? I need to get ready for work…"

"*Maddie.*" The voice came from the speaker end of the phone. It sounded dry and oozing at the same time. Again, "*Maddie… come back…*"

Maddie slammed her handset back onto its cradle. She knew the voice. It was the voice of the devil from her dream, the voice of the devil in that house.

She sat on her bed, looking at the clock—now with the correct time—and knew she had to leave for the plant.

"Please, Heavenly Father," she prayed, "let tomorrow be a better day."

***

Brandon reminded David that Mom was only working this shift during the summer and that, once school started, she would be coming home with them every day, with hugs and smiles, and even kisses on the cheek, if they weren't too old for that sort of thing. Brandon definitely was, but if David wasn't, that was okay. Mom was doing her best and they had plenty to eat and only a couple chores each. As Brandon washed their breakfast dishes and David shook out the kitchen rugs, Brandon did his best to be a good big brother.

"If you shake them in the middle of the floor, all that grimy stuff will be easier to sweep. Mom's gonna love that we swept; it's not on the list until tomorrow," Brandon said.

"Do you think Mom still loves us?" David asked, pausing his rug shaking. Small tears that Brandon hadn't noticed until now had formed in his eyes.

"David, yeah. Mom's always gonna love us, even if we act like jerks. It's part of being a mom."

"I know, but Dad never even calls and isn't it part of being a dad, too?"

"Dads sometimes are just different. I know a bunch of kids at school who don't have dads around anymore," Brandon said, now fighting tears of his own. Dad hadn't called in almost a year, not even on Brandon's birthday.

"It's not fair," David said, throwing the last rug down onto the floor. "I'm never going to be a dad if that's what happens. If I have kids, I'm never going to leave them."

"You'll be a great dad," Brandon said. "You'll be really great at picking up your kids' toys because you're great at picking up your own."

"Thanks," David said, wiping his cheeks and spreading a film of dust across his face.

"Now," Brandon said. "Do you want to sweep and I'll hold the dustpan?"

"No way! The broom is taller than me!"

***

Maddie wanted to call and check on her boys before they went to sleep, but she couldn't bear the thought of one of them answering the phone in her bedroom. She hung up the breakroom phone without dialing and rested her head against the wall until someone called her name.

"Hey, Maddie, you being a wallflower again?"

"What are you doing here now, Everett?" Maddie said, talking into the wall instead of to the man shed been promised she wouldn't have to see again while at work.

"Covering for Ronnie. He's sick or probably drunk. You know how those Jack Mormons are. A couple 3.2 beers and they're heaving their guts out."

"Leave me alone, Everett."

"Just saying *hi* is all, don't get your pantyhose bunched up."

"Go choke on your hello," Maddie said. The anger in her voice surprised her, but not as much as hearing a voice from inside her head but also from far away.

"*Yes, choke,*" the voice said.

Maddie looked away from the wall in time to see Everett toss a Lambert cherry into his mouth, take one bite, and start to gag. Small pieces of the dark-fleshed cherry popped out between his lips as he tried to gain air, but the pit remained hidden. She watched him choke until someone came up behind him and slapped him hard on the back. The pit flew out of Everett's mouth and landed by Maddie's feet.

"You don't get a pit spitting record if someone has to help you, Slocumb," said the person who rescued him.

Everett, usually always ready with a snappy comeback, said nothing. He stared at Maddie until he regained his breath, then backed out of the breakroom, only turning away from Maddie after he crossed the threshold.

Maddie, like Heather on the phone that afternoon, giggled like she had as a teenager with impure thoughts.

***

David only left Brandon's side once all afternoon and evening after doing their chores. If the sun went behind a cloud and a room went dark, David jumped. He told Brandon he was afraid the power would go out again and it scared him. Brandon didn't believe him. David routinely turned out the lights, sometimes before he left a room, and had never needed a night light. Brandon, however, still needed to know a nightlight was nearby, if not on. Brandon had kept a stuffed panda bear clutched against him until he was six and needed

Mom or Dad to stand by the door while he peed throughout kindergarten. David had always been the brave one.

Today, starting about an hour after Mom went to work, David followed Brandon around like a duckling trailing its mother duck. When Brandon had to take a dump after their pizza roll dinner, David sat against the wall outside the bathroom and would not shut up.

"I wonder why the power went out, don't you?" David said. "I wonder if anyone else's power went out. Do we have candles?"

"Can you just give me a minute?" Brandon said from inside the bathroom. The talking stopped, but Brandon could hear David tapping his fingers, then his fist, against the wall. The beating sound grew louder, making Brandon think David had stood up. He wiped and flushed, and then a louder, thicker smack banged against the wall. Brandon opened the door. David stood, his head back as if he was going to slam it into the wall. Again. His eyes were closed, as if he'd fallen asleep. David's body leaned, like someone held him by the back of the head and would soon splatter him against the wall.

"David!"

David didn't move. He didn't slump forward or lean back farther. He hovered there, his heels a pivot point on the floor. Brandon shouted again and saw his little brother's body loosen and crumble. He took the two steps needed to reach David and caught him as he collapsed to the ground.

The boys landed in a heap, younger on top of older.

"What are you doing down there?" David asked.

"Are you okay?" Brandon asked.

"Yeah, I think maybe I fell asleep while you were taking the world's longest crap. Is it bedtime yet?"

Brandon checked his watch, worn with the face on the inside of his wrist like his grandpa used to do. It wasn't quite eight o'clock, but if David wanted to go to bed, that was fine with him.

"Let's get some candles first, just in case," Brandon said.

Just for fun, Brandon lit one of the candles and put in on the nightstand between his bed and David's. He stared through the flame and at his brother, wondering if he should tell Mom about what happened. David said he didn't remember anything of the moments after he stopped talking up until he landed on Brandon in the hallway. The candle flickered and Brandon felt himself getting sleepy. He leaned over and blew the candle out.

When the knocking started, first light like finger tips then louder like a fist, Brandon was sure it was his mom stumbling in the dark while trying to be quite as she came home. He slowly opened his sleep-gunked eyes and saw the candle had been lit again. It had also been moved.

Sitting bolt upright and facing Brandon's bed, David held the candle in his lap on the floor. His eyes were closed but his lips moved. No sounds came out of David's mouth and even the way his lips formed the silent words looked strange to Brandon.

"Mom's going to be pissed you played with the lighter," Brandon said, finding something brave to say in the face of this mystery. "David. Blow that out and get back in bed."

David didn't stir. His lips stopped moving. Brandon crept forward, planning to put the candle out and get his brother back in bed. As he reached out, he felt something like a breeze touch his hand. Whatever touched him started to sting, like getting hit by a pin-point of forced air. He pulled his hand back. Another blast of air from nowhere snuffed out the candle. The hot candle rolled out of David's lap and onto the floor. Wax dripped onto the carpet.

The front door opened. Brandon could hear Maddie tripping over herself in the dark. He had to get David in bed before she reached their room.

He bounced out of bed, picked up the candle and put it on his dresser. Then, from behind, he hoisted his brother up into the bed. As Brandon pulled the covers back over David, David grabbed him and whispered into his ear.

"She's not safe," David said, never opening his eyes.

The boys' room smelled like burnt matches, and Maddie told herself to ask about it later. Brandon stirred in his bed, so she went no farther into the room. For now, she needed to sleep, too, and wonder about what happened to Everett Slocumb at work. *The boys must have had a candle out*, she thought. Preparing for the power to go out again. She closed the door, tip-toeing to her own room as day-old nightmares swirled in her mind. A fresh round of bad dreams awaited Maddie, but for tonight, she knew her boys were safe.

Chapter Four: Another Sunday Morning

For the next five days, Brandon prayed every morning that the weird things he saw on Tuesday were just a dream, or his imagination. Every day that went by without something odd happening, he believed it more and added that thankfulness to his prayers.

For the next five nights, Maddie prayed every evening that the dream of herself kneeling before the devil be taken away. She knew it was only a dream, but it made her feel sick. Sometimes, she dreamed she was watching the woman in the painting do … unnatural things… and she was thankful it wasn't her. She dreamt sometimes that the men in the painting made the woman disappear, sometimes all at once, occasionally piece by dismembered piece. These versions of the dream—the ones with the woman from the painting and not herself—also left her sick, but for a different reason. Maddie began to recognize the other woman.

Brandon served sacrament again. He was assigned the right side of the chapel. Maddie and David sat on the left side. Much of the congregation was absent, visiting family and such during the summer break. They'd be in their same clothes, sitting in a nearly identical chapel, singing songs from the same hymnal—maybe even the exact same songs—and doing things in the same order. For many, the structure of the Church of Jesus Christ of Latter-day Saints offered comfort. Every church building had a bold VISITORS WELCOME sign on it, and if you were a member, you could walk in and feel practically at home.

A wave of nausea came over Brandon as the blessing on the sacrament was spoken. He wasn't nervous that he'd mess up like the week before. He wasn't worried he would do something wrong. Instead, he felt like there was something right he needed to do and wasn't sure if he would be brave enough to act at the right time. It would help, he thought, if he knew what it was he was supposed to do.

He didn't notice during the passing of the bread—the body of Christ, broken—but as he and the other deacons passed the water—the blood of Christ, shed—his mother didn't take it. Two weeks in a row! Was that the thing he was supposed to do? Ask her why she'd not taken the sacrament for two weeks? Maybe he'd ask Bishop Griffen about it on Tuesday.

For his part, he felt a little better after taking his own bread and water.

Maddie fidgeted during the invocation, the opening hymn, and the announcements. During the sacrament hymn, she squirmed. Her skin seemed to go slack and then pull taut over and over. She tried focusing on Brandon, sitting reverently during the song and the blessing over the bread. She watched him pass his tray around as her body revolted. When David handed her the tray from another deacon, she reached for the handle instead of a piece of bread, held it for a moment, then handed it back to the young man. When he returned with the tray of water, she simply held up her hand. The deacon took back the tray after David replaced his empty cup.

She didn't see Brandon as he saw her refuse the sacrament. She only saw pulsating red and encroaching darkness.

The black stayed at the edges of her vision, the crimson at the center. The colors maintained position whether she moved her head or just her eyes: red and infusing ink. When people spoke to her, their faces were nearly blotted out by the scarlet hue and more than once someone snuck up on her because her peripheral vision remained blocked. Before she knew it, she had agreed to spend her night off carpooling with another family to Manti to see the Mormon Miracle Pageant. She hadn't been since she was young, which meant Brandon and David had never been. They deserved a night out and—she had to admit this was a bonus—it's free. As she shook hands, setting a place and time to meet on Wednesday, Bishop Griffen approached her.

As he came closer, the red in front of Maddie's eyes first grew and then dissipated. Some of the darkness clouding the edges of her sight lightened. A tightness in her chest loosened for a moment before reaffirming its grip. The moment was all she needed to take a deep breath and smile.

"Sister Smith, I was going to ask if you were feeling well, but you suddenly look ten times better than you did earlier," Bishop Griffen said, grasping her hand and wrist with his hands.

"Yes, Bishop, I've been under the weather, but the Christensens invited the boys and me to the pageant this week and it seems to have lifted my spirits."

"Good to hear, good to hear." He punctuated each phrase with a pump of Maddie's hand, then let go. "Don't forget, I'm meeting Brandon and then you on Tuesday."

"Yes, I remember."

"If you need anything before then and can't reach me, don't hesitate to call Elder Rasmussen or Brother Taylor. They're still assigned to your family, even with all the changes."

The changes, so many in the Church and in her home lately. A new Prophet and President, more temples, the new ministering program instead of home teachers... Dan Rasmussen and Larry Taylor had been Alex's home teachers and Maddie couldn't recall the last time they had visited her home. Her visiting teachers, Sisters Emma Rush and Dolores Sawyer, were also absorbed into the ministering program. Oh, and no more Boy Scout troop, but Brandon didn't seem too bothered by that. He would just keep rolling with the new and she hoped that attitude would continue.

"Yes," Maddie said. "I'll be sure to let them know."

"Tell your boys hello for me," Bishop Griffen said, now turning away to meet with other members of the congregation. As he broke eye contact and moved away from Maddie, her sight filled with an inky border and a circle of blood rose to obscure all in front of her. *I need to get back to working days*, she thought. *These swing and graveyards shift are killing me. That must be it.*

***

Maddie found a roast deep in the bottom of the chest freezer Saturday afternoon. "Use or freeze before 01/31/2018" was stickered on the plastic wrapping. She'd no doubt met the goal for freezing and as it was now late June, she hoped the meat would still be good. It looked okay to her after defrosting overnight and into the oven it went with some sliced carrots, potatoes, and onions. When the Smith family returned from church, the roast was done.

Her boys stripped off their white shirts and ties, both replacing them with superhero T-shirts. Before she could return from changing out of her own Sunday best, Brandon had dished up plates for everyone. She sat down and meant to tell the boys about being invited to the pageant when Brandon spoke up.

"We shouldn't forget to say a blessing for this meal," he

said. "I'll say it."

"Thank you, Brandon," Maddie said, wanting to be proud of her son but feeling that grip around her chest squeeze again.

"Dear Heavenly Father," Brandon began. "We thank Thee for the meal before us. Please bless this food that it will nourish and strengthen our bodies. Please, Father, also let it strengthen our minds and hearts to help us always remember Thy sacrifice for us and the love Thy son Jesus has for us. We say this in the name of Jesus. Amen."

David and Maddie said *amen,* but Maddie felt each word sting her, as if Brandon knew she had refused the sacrament that day and took it as an offense to himself and God. He didn't look at her again until he'd cleared his plate, give or take a carrot or two. When he did, his voice struck her like a slap.

"I'll clean up, Mom. Why don't you go rest."

She stood from the table, started to speak, closed her mouth as Brandon's determined gaze bore into her, and walked away. She closed her door behind her before the tears began.

"Mom's crying. Why did you make Mom cry?" David asked.

"I didn't mean to," Brandon said. "I was just trying to help, and knew she'd just say not to if I didn't say it a bit harder."

"Dad used to make her cry like that."

"I'm not Dad. Now, are you going to help me do the dishes or should I do them alone?"

"I'll dry."

They washed in relative silence, with David humming a primary song every other dish. Maddie's cries died out before they finished the silverware. As David put away the roast pan —the last dish of the day—Maddie emerged from her room and sat in the same chair she had vacated and watched her boys wipe down the counters and spray away the soap bubbles from the sink.

"Boys," she said, holding her arms wide. They turned and came to her. She enveloped them both in a hug she wished to never let go of.

"I'm sorry, Mom," Brandon said. "I didn't mean to."

"You're fine, Brandon. It's fine." She released them from the embrace but held a hand in each of hers. "Do you want to go to Manti on Wednesday and see the pageant?"

A chorus of yeses erupted from the boys and they returned the hug given them earlier. Brandon, leaning in closer, whispered "Thank you" into Maddie's ear.

"I'll need lots of help around the house between now and then. Just like you helped today."

"Yes, Mom," Brandon and David said together.

"Good. Now go play outside or something. I have to get ready for work."

Chapter Five: Sunday Night/Monday Morning

Maddie signed whatever birthday cards or anniversary cards, or any other greetings were left in the breakroom at the cherry plant during the summer or the teacher's lounge during the school year. There was always a pen, so signing took zero effort. How many times had she casually scrawled Wishing you the best or Thinking of you today and her name? She picked up the latest, a Get Well card, and began to jot her halfhearted but well-intentioned addition before seeing whom the card was for. As she stared at the salutation carefully written above a printed message extolling the recipient to look on the bright side, a hand fell on her shoulder.

"I didn't think you'd be signing a card for Everett," Roberta from the day shift said.

"What do you mean?" Maddie asked, remembering Everett choking when she saw him less than a week ago.

"You aren't the only gal he came at, honey."

Maddie relaxed, not hearing the accusatory tone she expected from Roberta. "Do you know what's wrong with him?"

"Heard something about a breathing spell a couple days ago. Collapsed lung or something. Been in Foothill View almost a week."

Go choke on your hello, shed said to Everett and he'd choked on a cherry pit when the voice in her head agreed with her. And now, a breathing spell or a collapsed lung. Choking on nothing but air. The red spot shed been able to ignore all afternoon pulsed. Instead of making her feel ill, she let the pulse wash over her. The more she gave into it, the clearer her vision became. The tint didn't disappear, but rather infiltrated her sight in a way that made it less noticeable, like wearing sunglasses that weren't dark enough to make it difficult to see but still blocked out the light.

"How awful for him," Maddie said to Roberta. She smiled and started her signature over: *Wishing you all the fresh air you deserve, M.*

She smiled her entire shift and spoke to three more women who were equally pleased that something bad had happened to Everett Slocumb.

***

Brandon couldn't sleep. At first, he couldn't sleep because David tossed and turned, moaning and grinding his teeth like he did after their dad first left. Back then, Brandon would try to comfort him, or Maddie would come into the room if she was home and hold the younger Smith boy until he finally drifted away to dreamland. Brandon started to crawl out of his bed in order to settle his brother with the hope of getting some shut eye for both of them. Seeing David's eyes wide open, but still making his struggling sleep noises, stopped Brandon cold.

When David threw off his covers and began to float, Brandon retreated under his blankets and, like a turtle hiding in its shell, watched his little brother hover six inches above his bed, hands stiff at his sides, finally silent. Brandon stared, also unable to move, until the first rays of dawn peeked around the curtains and into the room.

He kept the vigil so long that he didn't realize his

mother never came in to check on them as she always did when she returned home from work. Brandon began to cry as more light found its way into the room and David slowly descended back onto his mattress. He watched as David contacted the bed, found his blankets, covered himself and rolled over, blessedly facing away from Brandon.

Both boys remained in their beds until Maddie came in to tell them she'd made pancakes.

"Did you make me a Mickey?" David shouted with glee, as if he had slept without problem and was on fire to face the day.

"I sure did. I made some of Brandon's favorites, too," Maddie said.

"Space cakes?" asked David.

"All moons!"

Brandon couldn't share the laughter at this old joke. He knew something was wrong with his brother and the look in his mother's eyes made him think something was wrong with her, too. He didn't know how to be the only right person in the house.

He took a deep breath and began to cough. Black spots swarmed in his eyes and he thought he was going to pass out.

"Come get a drink, kiddo," Maddie shouted to him from the kitchen. "Sounds like you could use some water."

His coughing fit calmed as he walked into the kitchen. David sat at the table, devouring a pancake covered in maple syrup that now had only one ear and half its head left. A plate of pancakes waited at Brandon's usual spot, also dripping with butter but no syrup, as he preferred.

"I brought home some fresh cherry syrup," Maddie said. "Thought you might like it." She took a small jar and poured a clotted mess of red over his pancakes. As it mixed with the butter and found the pores of the cakes, the red appeared to bubble. After his sleepless night and still feeling lightheaded from coughing, Brandon thought his pancakes were bleeding.

To Brandon, his fall to the floor seemed to take hours.

To Maddie, watching her son crumble to the ground went by in seconds.

Voices surrounded Brandon, but he couldn't see anyone. He knew it was daytime, but everything was as dark as the middle of the night. Something heavy and moist pressed against his eyes, preventing him from opening them. He reached up and felt a wet wash cloth covering his face. He pulled the cloth off and opened one eye at a time. David sat next to him, his face in his hands. He could see Maddie talking with two men on the other side of the room. One of the men wore blue jeans but both had on crisp white shirts. Brandon guessed they were wearing ties, too, which meant they were from church.

Brandon grunted, trying to hoist himself into a better position. Before he found a comfortable spot, David shouted.

"Mom! Brandon's awake!"

"David, shhh. There's no need to yell," Maddie said. She came to the couch and kneeled on the floor. "How you feeling?"

"Thirsty," Brandon said. "Fine, just thirsty."

"Okay. I'll get you some water. You sure you don't feel sick or anything?"

"I'm sure."

When Maddie returned, the two men were at her sides.

"Brandon, do you remember Elder Rasmussen and Brother Taylor from church?"

Brandon nodded while sipping from his glass.

"They're going to give you a blessing, just in case, okay?"

"Okay," Brandon said.

They'd all had blessings when Dad left. Blessings to help them remain faithful and strong. Brandon wasn't entirely sure they worked, but he did his best to believe. He sat up and moved from the couch to a kitchen chair that had been set in the middle of the room. One of the men—Rasmussen, Brandon thought—poured oil on his head from a small vial and said a quick prayer. Then both men had their hands on top of Brandon's head.

Brandon, who always prayed with his eyes closed tight, kept his eyes open as the men prayed over him. Between the men, he could see his mother. She sat on the couch next to David, but as the blessing continued, she seemed to fade in and out to Brandon. He concentrated harder on her instead of on the words being prayed over him and watched as she disappeared and reappeared looking like a different woman. Next to her, David seemed to turn red, then black, then red again. He appeared to crumble away like paint from an old house before returning to normal. The appearance of the strange woman melted away from Maddie and she appeared to be herself again, too.

I've ruined everything, he thought. I'm *sick and we'll have to move into... I don't want to move!*

"...and this we pray in the name of Jesus Christ. Amen," Taylor said, concluding the blessing. They removed their hands from Brandon's head and then took turns shaking his hand.

"You should be fine, but if anything happens, don't hesitate to see a doctor, too," Rasmussen said.

"We won't," Maddie said, standing from the couch and escorting the men to the door. "Thank you for coming so quickly."

She shut the door as the men said their goodbyes.

"How long was I knocked out, Mom?" Brandon asked.

"About half an hour, but then you seemed to need to sleep, so I got you to the couch. It's almost two and I still need to get to work. Do you think you'll be okay?"

"Yeah, I just didn't sleep well last night, is all."

"Okey-dokey, honey, You'll get some extra rest," Maddie said. "Sister Rasmussen is going to bring over something for dinner and I rescheduled our bishop appointments tomorrow for next week."

Brandon felt a need to argue against that, to meet with Bishop Griffen right away, but if his mom had already changed the meeting, then there wasn't much he could do. He had to concentrate on watching his brother and looking forward to a night in Manti instead. "Okay, Mom, if you think that's best."

"I do. I love you both. Ill try to get off work early." She kissed Brandon on the forehead and David on the cheek before walking out the door.

***

Later, after eating part of the lasagna Sister Rasmussen brought over, David tugged on Brandon's shirt like he did when he was little and wanted something.

"Brandon, I found something in Mom's room," David said.

"You know you aren't supposed to go in there."

"I know, but look." David handed his older brother a real estate flier. In full color, the house on 600 North announced itself as being **FOR SALE OR RENT** and listed its various features. The flier looked sunbaked and the text was faded. Folds creased it like someone had stuffed it in their pocket. The photograph of the house still looked crisp and almost freshly printed. "Here, you have it. I've had it for a few days. What does it mean?"

"Where'd you get it?

"I found it in Mom's room. It was right there. I had it in my pocket the other day, but it felt itchy, so I put it under my mattress last night. I had bad dreams about it all night. Do you think it's a real house here in Blackhawk?"

Brandon didn't want to touch the piece of paper, so he went to the kitchen and got some tongs from a drawer, then took the flier from his brother. "Yeah, it's a real house, it has to be. Has the address right there. And there are a bunch of these old houses in town."

David shook and then steadied. "We should check it out," he said in a voice that to Brandon seemed older than his brother's nine-year-old voice.

"I don't think so. Plus, it's on the other side of town. You can't ride your bike that far."

"I don't want to go," said David, sounding closer to his age. "It looks spooky."

"Just throw it away. Somebody probably left it on Mom's car at work." Brandon started to take the flier to the trash under the kitchen sink, but instead went to the back door and put it in the big can outside. He didn't know why, but he didn't want it in the house anymore.

Chapter Six: The Pageant and the Grove

Two nights of dream-free sleep left the Smith family refreshed and ready for the trip to Manti. They all slept in Wednesday morning, ate a huge lunch at home, then went to Walmart to get supplies for the journey. They'd get hungry and thirsty on the drive and since they could bring in food for the late pageant, Maddie decided to go for more hoagies. They'd bring the meats and cheeses and the Christensens would bring the buns and chips. After a few household chores—Brandon washing and drying the dishes, David sweeping the kitchen, taking out the trash, and cleaning up around the garbage cans—they were ready to go.

The Christensens—Alan, Amy and their two girls Aiden and Amanda—arrived at the Smith home at four o'clock. "That way we won't have to fight as hard for a place to park this beast," Alan Christensen said, slapping the dashboard of his Chevy Suburban.

Brandon laughed, not at Brother Christensen, but at something his mom had said once, pointing out the huge SUV in the church parking lot: *There goes another Mormon assault vehicle, doing the Lord's work.*

"Don't encourage his jokes," Sister Christensen said. "They'll only get worse."

"She's not kidding," said Aiden, a thirteen-year-old blonde, sitting on the left side of the car. Her sister, seven, sat next to her, then David. Brandon sat with Maddie in the middle row.

Many jokes, one spilled can of Sprite, and some sisterly name calling later, they arrived in Manti and at the foot of the temple. The cream-colored building stood on a hill, looking down on everything else in the valley. Some temples frightened Brandon, either because the buildings looked needlessly dark or too pointy, but the Manti temple, where his grandparents had been married for time and eternity, soothed him. He looked at his watch and wished his grandpa could be with him.

Alan Christensen found a space not too far from the entrance gate and turned off the car. Everyone unloaded, each taking a plastic bag with them.

"Looks like we'll get a good spot in the chairs, too," Amy Christensen said.

A couple hundred people milled about around the gate, waiting for it to open. Across the street, a gathering of protesters stood with signs. Brandon soon realized that not all the people with signs were together. Those holding signs claiming there was only one way to Jesus and Mormons weren't it were arguing with another group holding rainbow-colored signs. They didn't seem to like each other, but they all had something against the Mormons. As they walked by, Brother Christensen shouted.

"The pageant is free, folks, you should come in and learn something."

"Get bent, polygamist," a round old woman shouted. Brother Christensen just waved, and the two families walked through the gate onto the south lawn of Temple Hill.

The first rows were filled, but the group of seven found a spot in the fourth row that gave them the best view of the expanse of the lawn and the wall jutting out from the back of the 130-year-old building. After they haggled over who would sit where—Brandon played it cool but was happy when he ended up next to Aiden—they got out the food and started a sandwich assembly line. Aiden's hands lightly grazed Brandon's each time she passed something to him and he did his best to ignore it. They ate as more people filled in the seats behind them, all chatting away, creating a cacophony of voices in which nothing could be understood.

The crowd began to settle as the sun met the horizon. Brandon watched David begin to nod off and more than once jostled him awake. Even Brother and Sister Christensen had glazed looks in their eyes. Only Maddie looked fully awake.

Brandon—and he assumed most of the people in the crowd—knew the story that would soon unfold before him. In 1820, in New York State, a boy named Joseph Smith sought clarification on which church to join. In a vision, he saw Heavenly Father and Jesus Christ, who told him that none of the churches were the true church, as Christ formed it during his time on earth. A series of angelic visitations led to the discovery of golden plates that contained the story of a primitive people, ancient Jews, who fled Israel and settled in North and Central America. Joseph Smith published the translated story as *The Book of Mormon* in 1830 and started the Church of Jesus Christ of Latter-day Saints. The new church members faced persecution and fled west to Ohio, then Illinois, and finally to the land out west they called Deseret, which became Utah and a state in the Union in 1896. Along the way, in 1844, Joseph Smith was martyred.

Brandon couldn't remember the first time he had heard this story. It was a part of his life and Brandon accepted it. According to Maddie, Brandon's father Alex came from a line of Joseph Smith's relatives, but she added that there were so many Smiths in Utah that they couldn't possibly all be related.

***

"There are so many Smiths in Utah, we can't possibly all be related," Maddie said to Sister Christensen just as bright lights illuminated the wide, green lawn. Night had finally come and the pageant, the history of their religion, was about to play out in front of them.

Maddie remembered how colorful the costumes of the Nephites and Lamanites—the ancient tribes who wrote on the original golden plates—had been when her parents brought her here as a child. She didn't expect them to be as spectacular now, as nothing over the last two years, even, she admitted, before Alex left, had been that spectacular. She wouldn't admit to any sort of depression, but shed watched her mother slide into doldrums from time to time and knew what they were. The red blur that had clouded her vision had mostly faded and she was happy to see her children enjoying themselves. Brandon couldn't keep the smile off his face at being able to sit so closely to Aiden, even though she could tell he was trying to be cool. *Cool guys end up being the worst*, she thought. *Your dad was cool. Just be yourself.*

In this lawn chair, at the sacred place, she could sit and bask in remembrance of better times when she'd drive here and not have to wear a seatbelt, sometimes even sleeping in the space between the backseat and the back window. She thought of how amazing it was that a teenager in New York could start something so big that it was worldwide and would bring 15,000 people out late on a weeknight.

Maddie tried to say a prayer of thankfulness for the moment, but couldn't. She watched as the young man playing Joseph Smith kneeled to pray for guidance and then writhed on the lawn, the narrator stating that the boy was under a spiritual attack while seeking knowledge from God in a grove of trees, praying in a small clearing. The soft lights shining on the actor flickered and grew dark. The cloud at the edges of Maddie's vision surged and covered her eyes in darkness.

She found herself kneeling in the clearing, the

moonlight above her, voices behind her. Looking toward the moon, she could see a house that didn't belong at the edge of a forest but was right where it needed to be. She was in the painting, but this didn't feel like a dream.

The three men behind her chanted a name, but it wasn't Maddie's. She knew the name from somewhere. Some friend of a friend? Someone Alex knew? Someone from high school in Blackhawk?

Then she remembered what happened in the painting and in her dreams. The Maddie in the grove began to scream and try to stand.

The Maddie sitting in a lawn chair at the Mormon Miracle Pageant also began to scream and tried to stand. Her arms flew out in front of her and her legs kicked out. Her right arm belted Sister Christensen in the mouth, drawing blood. A foot connected against the back of a man in a suit in front of her and forced him out of his chair. Brother Christensen leapt over his wife to try to restrain Maddie and caught her foot in his crotch. He went down and barely avoided getting kicked in the eye.

Brandon and David saw the commotion, too. David sat and began to cry. "Mommy, what's wrong?" he said through his tears.

Brandon stepped on Brother Christensen and fell into Sister Christensen trying to get to Maddie. Once he was clear of them, getting a good smear of Sister Christensen's bleeding mouth on his shirt, he was able to grab Maddie's arms and embrace her in a way that kept her arms still and forced her to sit and stop kicking.

"Mom. Mommy, what's wrong?" Brandon said. Her eyes remained closed.

In the clearing, Maddie felt her son's arms wrapping around her and tried to focus on his voice. *Mommy, what's wrong?* she heard. There were other noises and perhaps an ambulance siren. The men who had been chanting behind her were no longer there. She must have screamed loud enough that the devil never appeared before her, but she knew something she didn't know before.

In Manti, Maddie opened her eyes, saw the chaos around her, and began to weep. Brandon held her close; David stood nearby. The Christensens huddled a few yards away, an EMT shining a light at Sister Christensen's mouth. She had to tell Brandon what she knew before something happened and made her forget.

"Samantha Robinson is in that house. The devil took her, and he wants me," Maddie whispered in Brandon's ear. Then she closed her eyes again. Her head slumped to one side and her body became lax in her oldest son's arms.

"She's passed out!" Brother Christensen yelled, grabbing an EMT by the shoulder. "Maddie's passed out. Help her."

Brandon knew exactly what house Maddie meant. He would find out who Samantha Robinson was and help his mom. He would beat the devil. He had to. His mom needed him. He thought about the flier he'd thrown away and that made him think of David floating above his bed. *I wish I still had my appointment with Bishop Griffen*, he thought and a painful warmth went up his spine. He shook it off and returned his thoughts to his mom.

Part Two:
Meadows

"And in the name of Jesus did he cast out devils and unclean spirits; and even his brother did he raise from the dead, after he had been stoned and suffered death by the people."

3 Nephi 7:19, *The Book of Mormon*

Chapter Seven: Pioneer Day

The bishop of the Blackhawk Third Ward had visited Maddie Smith two or three times a week for the last month without event. He walked into the home that he had arranged payments for through the end of the year, and every Friday he brought in a few groceries to help supplement what he was able to provide via the Bishop's Storehouse shortly after Maddie became bedridden. The two boys in the house seemed to survive mostly on cereal during the day, which meant they needed plenty of milk.

Blaine Griffen had been ordained as the bishop the prior summer, just after retiring from a career in academic advising. He'd seen his institution go from a community college to a state college and finally to a full university offering a handful of graduate degrees. More than once over the last thirty years he had consoled an incoming freshman over their disappointment at not being accepted at Brigham Young University, the church-operated university a few miles away. This is a good school, he'd say, and you'll get a great education at about half the price. His retention rate was only one of the reasons he'd lasted thirty years and through so many changes.

His short time as bishop showed him a whole new world of changes. Political divisions widened, people who seemed like they'd live in Blackhawk forever moved, children were exposed to horrible things on television and the internet, and drugs were everywhere. He expected a few potheads, some kids who got a beer from an older friend, that sort of stuff. He didn't expect to see so many fathers abusing painkillers and mothers reliant on anti-depressants just to get through the day. Every day, the world reminded Griffen of its brokenness.

He stood inside a home now living out that brokenness. He had known Alex Smith and Maddie was one of the first people he saw after becoming bishop. She was in pain then, still dealing with her husband leaving. He helped her see the hope in her children. Why she hadn't come to him sooner about the trouble with her house payments, he didn't know. For now, the house remained hers. For now, something far worse was happening to her.

Most of the time, Maddie laid stiff in her bed, arms rigid by her sides, toes straight up. She ignored almost everyone who came into the room, whether it was sisters from the Relief Society or priesthood members who visited to give her blessings and pray over her. Her own boys hadn't seen her since she took to bed.

But things were different with the bishop. When she greeted him the first time he visited, the others in the room thought she'd be fine and would soon be talking with everyone. Instead, she only addressed Griffen.

"Good morning, Blaine," Maddie said as he entered her room.

"Hello, Sister Smith, how are you today?"

She didn't move but appeared to momentarily elongate. Griffen took off his glasses and rubbed his eyes. When he put them back on, she was in the middle of the bed, as she had been every time he saw her over the past four weeks.

"Good as ever. Ready to die," she said.

"Not today. Sister Christensen and Sister Young are coming to see you. I'm taking your boys over to Spanish Fork along with some other kids from the ward to enjoy the carnival. We've already missed the parade, but there'll be another next year."

"They love the rides. Gravitron, the Ferris wheel, the Scrambler…"

"There's a new one this year. Some wild shaking thing they call Earthquake."

Maddie's eyes opened and she looked at Griffen. Her face exploded into a smile, blood filling in the cracks of her dried lips. "*Terromoto.*"

Griffen took his glasses off again, sweat forming on his forehead. He coughed, cleared his throat, and as calmly as he could, said, "I didn't know you knew Spanish, Sister Smith."

Maddie's eyes rolled into her head, exposing the whites. Still smiling, blood now covering her teeth, she said, "There's so much you don't know." A single, barking laugh escaped from her. Her eyes closed and her body regained the stiffened posture Griffen had become accustomed to.

He walked out of her room, softly closing the door behind him. David greeted him, a small smile on his face.

"I wish Mom could come to the carnival with us," the boy said.

"Yes, so do I. But your mother needs more rest. I am sure she will be well soon," Griffen said, putting his hand on David's shoulder. "You and your brother have been very brave for her. Heavenly Father needs you to keep being brave, okay?"

"Yes, Bishop. We will."

He took David by the hand and walked toward the front door. Brandon waited near the door but didn't look happy to be leaving the house.

"Brandon, is something troubling you?" Griffen said.

"Only everything. Bishop, could we make a stop on the way to the carnival?"

***

Following Brandon's directions, Bishop Griffen pulled in front of the sandstone Victorian on 600 North. "This is in the 11th Ward, Brandon," Griffen said. "Arthur Morrison is the bishop these days. Good man of God."

"Uh huh," Brandon said, staring at the house his mother had a flier for. He still didn't know why she'd have an ad for a house for rent, but he wasn't stupid. "Bishop, do you think Mom is going to move us here?"

Before Griffen could answer, David chimed in. "I don't want to move. Can we go? I don't like it here."

"Boys, your mother is facing many challenges right now. What she needs from you both is your strength and your faith in her and Heavenly Father. The Church and I are doing our best to make sure you don't have to move for as long as possible."

Brandon took this in, accepting that his family would eventually move out of the Third Ward and maybe even out of Blackhawk, and hoped that they wouldn't move into this house. "Let's go," he said. "I don't like it here, either."

Bishop Griffen started his car, which gave an uncharacteristic chugging before firing up, and took the Smith boys to meet with other kids at the carnival in Spanish Fork.

For a moment, maybe thirty minutes, Brandon tried to forget about his mom and whatever weird sickness had befallen her. He tried to push aside his worries about the old house and his suspicion that Maddie had gone in there and something inside made her sick. And whatever had made her sick might be contagious. Asbestos, perhaps, like he'd hear about on the news when one of the older buildings in Salt Lake City was being renovated or torn down, or some weird germ like in that old movie they filmed at the corn lab near West Mountain.

He tried to just have fun, and he almost did, until he

saw Bishop Griffen standing in front of the Earthquake ride. Griffen's hands were jammed deep into his pockets and he looked the opposite of how Brandon felt, like he was trying to remember something instead of forget things, as Brandon had been doing. Griffen's mouth was moving. To Brandon, it looked like he was muttering the same word over and over, but Brandon couldn't hear it among the chaos of the carnival.

Brandon took a step toward the bishop, but David came up behind him and grabbed his hand.

"Come ride the Gravitron, Brandon" David shouted. "There's no line right now!"

Bishop Griffen turned his head and smiled at Brandon. David pulled his big brother's hand until he relented. The boys rode the Gravitron until they ran out of tickets.

When they exited the ride for the last time, they saw Bishop Griffen with a group of kids from their ward near the snow cone stand. As they rushed to the stand, Brandon noticed three men watching him and his brother. He didn't know them, but they seemed vaguely familiar, like faces you see in a dream and then see during the day. When he reached the snow cone stand, he turned back to point the men out to Bishop Griffen, but they were gone.

***

In her room, a chill startled Maddie away from the sleep she nearly reached. She longed for the dark, for a dreamless rest. The wave of cold that roused her started in her toes. It shivered up her legs and through her torso, down her arms, and somehow back into her head. She pulled her thick quilt—one her grandmother had tied at a Daughters of the Utah Pioneers meeting—up to her ears. The cold lingered like a cloud surrounding her skull. It pressed into her eyes and filled her nostrils. Her sinuses felt like ice cubes inside her face.

And then it all melted. The chill became a viscous liquid fire as it ran into her throat, choking her. She sat up, coughing and gagging. Black tar poured from her nose and mouth and more leaked out her ears. The lower half of her face was engulfed in the dark slime and she felt as though the flood of murky fire would never end. She could not scream out as the bile poured from her mouth.

Who would she scream to, anyway? Bishop Griffen had taken her children. She was alone in her room, alone in the world.

I am here, Maddie.

"Who…?"

She knew the voice without having ever heard it out loud. It was not the still, small voice of the Holy Ghost she had too often ignored. It was the voice of the painting.

Maddie, I am here and you are mine now.

The voice was inside her head, flowing with the black tar, and outside, coming from the corner farthest from any hint of light. Each syllable sounded like a croaking toad. Between every word, a chirping like angry crickets, filled the space. She looked toward the place she thought the voice came from and saw shuffling shadows but no distinct shapes. She coughed a ragged, death-rattle cough and her throat cleared of the muck.

"Get out of my head and out of my house," she said.

This house, too, shall be mine.

At first, only the bed shook. Then the dresser and the full-length mirror. The closet doors rattled in their frame. The photographs on the dresser tipped over and Maddie cried at the sound of shattering glass. The drawers flew open and slammed shut.

At my will, not His, I shall make the earth tremble. Before me all shall kneel and forget the one who calls Himself savior. My shadow shall be cast over all the earth for a millennium.

Maddie gripped her quilt as the mattress beneath her rocked back and forth, threatening to spill her to the floor. The convulsions launched her into the air, where she hovered for a moment before reconnecting to the weight of the mattress. She clasped her hands together and did her best to pray, still coughing on remnants of black filth.

"Dear Heavenly Father, please make this stop. Remove this evil from me and my house. Please, Lord. I pray in the name of Your son, Jesus Christ. Amen."

No reply came. Her coughing ceased. The room fell still and silent again. She thought to get up and wash away the slime that had emptied out of her face but saw no trace of it on her quilt. She touched her chin, expecting to feel the stickiness that had enveloped her, but touched only her skin, a small patch of acne from lack of proper care over the previous weeks. She closed her eyes and lay back down. The weight of the quilt comforted her as she slipped into quiet sleep.

It's over, Maddie thought. *Whatever that was, it's over.*

In the corner of her room, the shadows coalesced into a solid form. Arms and legs grew from the center, eyes darker than the rest of the shadow opened. Horns sprouted from the top. The form moved, slowly stalking to Maddie's bed. It lay down beside her, then disappeared into her. She stirred a bit, but remained asleep.

A small sleep-whisper, like a toad at twilight, escaped her lips: *I am here for you, Maddie.*

A knock at the front door didn't rouse Maddie. The sisters waited to see if Maddie would answer on her own before using the spare key Bishop Griffen had given them. They entered a home that was as well-kept as a home with two young boys could be. A cursory glance at each room gave Sister Christensen and Sister Young everything they needed to perform their neighborly duties. While Sister Young cleaned, avoiding only Maddie's bedroom for now, Sister Christensen prepared a week's worth of dinners and placed them in the freezer.

With those tasks completed, the sisters went together to check on Maddie. Sister Christensen opened the door and walked in. Sister Young followed and went immediately to the closet and closed the doors. Nothing seemed out of place. Brandon and David smiled from the photos on the dresser, the full-length mirror stood upright, and Maddie herself appeared snug as a bug beneath her quilt, as Sister Young would say when reporting to Bishop Griffen the next day.

Neither woman noticed the small pool of black sludge beneath Maddie's bed.

***

On the drive home, after the other kids had been dropped off, Brandon took the front seat next to Bishop Griffen.

"You sure didn't like the look of that Earthquake ride, Bishop," Brandon said. "Too scary?"

"Yeah, it put a shock in me, son," Griffen said. "Does your mom know Spanish?"

"I'm sure she's picked some up. One year, she had six kids from Mexico in her class. Even David can count to ten in Spanish."

"Good point. Has she ever talked in Spanish at home?"

"No. Dad used to. He'd do a dumb accent and just say *tacos* or *fajitas* and some other words Mom told me never to say out loud. I don't know what they meant which means they must be swears."

"You're probably right about that."

"Does that have something to do with the ride, Bishop?"

"Yes and no. I know you haven't spent a lot of time with your mother since she's been in bed so much, but I need you to do me a favor. Can you, son?"

"Sure."

"I need you to listen for anything she says that sounds like another language. Like Spanish or anything you don't understand."

"Okay," Brandon said, his concerns about his mom flooding back into the forefront of his thought. "Should I write them down or anything? I have a recorder I'm allowed to use in certain classes. I could use that."

"That would be great. If you hear anything odd, let me know."

They pulled up to the Smith home just as Sisters Christensen and Young were about to lock the door behind them.

"All finished, sisters?" Bishop Griffen asked. He shook hands with each woman and helped them to Sister Christensen's car.

"She's resting easy, Bishop," Sister Young said. Then, looking at David and Brandon, she said, "Try to keep things clean in there. There's food in the freezer with cooking instructions. Just follow the directions. Your mom is asleep, so let her be."

"We will," Brandon said.

The women left and Bishop Griffen put a hand on each boy's shoulder. "Remember to pray for your mom, boys. Heavenly Father loves you and has a plan. Keep that mind."

"Yes, Bishop," the boys replied.

He let them go. Brandon looked back one last time.

"I won't forget what you asked me, Bishop."

"Good, son, good." As Brandon closed the door behind him, Bishop Blaine Griffen wondered exactly what had befallen Maddie Smith and why she would say the one word that sent his heart racing and his head throbbing. He knew who to call to help him figure it out.

Chapter Eight: And it Came to Pass

Rey Montoya poured over papers he had to handle with white cotton gloves and others that were mere copies of documents recording activities of the man who started the religion he had devoted his life to. Joseph Smith's written life lay before him, all the contradictions and corroborated facts, the truths that only other members of the Church of Jesus Christ of Latter-day Saints believed.

More than once, on his mission in Chile and even here in Utah, the question of truth and belief confronted him. If this is true, if Heavenly Father and His Son Jesus Christ directed Joseph Smith to re-establish the one true church in America, why was there so much conflict and confusion surrounding that truth?

Even the best people are human and full of human weaknesses, Montoya once told a young man as the teenager questioned his duty to go on a mission. *And Satan is the great deceiver who preys upon our weaknesses.*

You say that like Satan is a real person, the young Grant Taysom said and even though Montoya wished he didn't know the truth, he couldn't lie to this soldier of Christ.

Satan, son, is more real than I hope you will ever have to know, Montoya told him.

Some of the papers laid out before Montoya came to him via the now grown Taysom. Like Montoya, he wasn't so young any more. Both worked for the church, Montoya serving as the stake president in Blackhawk and his younger friend as an archivist at church headquarters in Salt Lake City. Montoya, a convert in his teens, devoted through a mission in another country, a marriage to an equally devout woman who preceded him in death, and all the baby blessings, baptisms, confirmations, temple sealings, and funerals that come with a large Mormon family, reached out to his junior friend for specific stories about Smith and his time as God's prophet on Earth.

"It's like Google, President Montoya," the archivist had said. "You need to play around with your search terms. So, nothing came up with your original word choice. I asked around, which got me called into my supervisor's office, and found the word you needed."

"What word is that?" Montoya had asked.

"Dispossession, although the more generic 'casting out' is much more common."

Montoya played the word over in his head. It had a modern, clean sound to it. More like the dark suits and white shirts of LDS men than the flowing robes and purple and gold stoles of the Catholics Montoya grew up with in New Mexico.

Dispossession: sterile, down-to-business, nose to the grindstone. A worker bee's word. Not at all like exorcism.

***

Griffen, Montoya's former mission companion in Chile, stared at his old friend's number on his phone, hesitating to push **CALL** and open a chest of horrors he'd buried four decades ago. Standing outside Maddie Smith's house after dropping off her boys, Griffen trembled. The tremors running down his arms threatened to shake the phone out of his hands. His thumb brushed the icon for his photo album and all the horror flooded back into him.

The photo he snapped minutes before, trying to get some proof that he wasn't imagining the extent of the tragedy inside the Smith home, stared at him with three faces. Maddie Smith, tortured and enduring unimaginable pain; Maricela, the face from forty-five years before, the girl they couldn't save, covered in flames and screaming out her unearned damnation; and the third, behind the faces of the women, built of torment and fire, the face of the devil laughing at Griffen.

He turned off the phone and decided to drive to Montoya's. He would explain everything better in person.

By then, perhaps the smell would be out of his nose.

***

The smell, Griffen told Montoya, assaulted him immediately upon entering the house. The boys smelled it, too. If they hadn't, Griffen would have been sure he was insane.

"We used to light cow patties on fire out in the pasture when I was a kid," Griffen said. "They burned low and hotter than you'd think. Too much heat, not enough light, and something trying to crawl down your throat and up your nose so that you'd rather be blind and cold instead of covered with that odor."

"Thanks for bringing it here," Montoya said. "What happened next?"

"Next," Griffen said, now seated on Montoya's sofa beneath a painting of Jesus cradling a black lamb. "Next, I saw Hell again."

"Again…"

"Yeah, like Chile. That's why I came to you."

Montoya's thoughts drifted to the documents he had been reading before his old companion showed up at his door. Stories of the prophet Joseph Smith casting out demons like Jesus and the apostles did in the New Testament.

Taysom had found the stories that confirmed the experience Montoya and Griffen had shared in Santiago, although Smith had been more successful in his dispossessions than they had been, even as early as 1830 when the prophet expelled a demon from a man named Newel Knight with just the touch of his hand.

"Once I could tolerate the smell," Griffen said, bringing Montoya back into the present, "and wiped the sweat from my face, I went into her room. I told the boys to stay in the living room."

He had to demand Brandon and David stay in the living room, to not follow him into their mother's bedroom. The foul odor of burning excrement lingered most heavily in the rooms and halls leading to the master bedroom. A light like a space heater glowed from beneath the door and Griffen was certain he would burn his hands if he pushed open the door. But when he grasped the knob, his fingers chilled. He placed his other hand on the door and felt a coldness in direct opposition to the oppressive heat in the rest of the house. He pushed against the door, turning the knob, but met resistance. A groan of distress emanated from behind the door so Griffen pushed harder. The door crashed open and for a split second, Griffen wished he'd not opened it.

He saw a mostly empty room, scant light slipping in between the boards that built the room, a mattress against the far wall and a prostrate form upon it, writhing in pain.

Squashing his eyes closed, Griffen prayed.

"Oh, Heavenly Father, take this vision away. It's 2018, not 1973. Lord, thou knowest we did what we could. Let this be different. I pray in the name of Thy son Jesus Christ. Amen."

Slowly, he let his eyes see again. The walls solidified but the room remained dimly lit. The bed had moved to the center of the room and wasn't flat on the floor. The thing that had not changed, the squirming, twitching body on the bed, sent the chilliness of the room deep into Griffen's heart.

Maddie Smith lay face down, but her arms stretched to the ceiling and her legs pointed outward, each finger and toe shivering with a life of its own. She let out a howl that should have been muffled by the pillow her face ground into, but instead shattered any silence left in the home. Two pairs of feet came running toward Griffen. He was glad for the chance to turn away from what he saw.

"Stay back, boys," he shouted, hands outs to the sprinting sons of the woman on the bed. "This is not for you to see."

The boys stopped in their tracks. David whispered out, "Mommy?"

"I'll take care of her, David. For now, Brandon will take care of you. Back to the other room, now!"

Brandon wrapped his arms around his little brother but looked back over his shoulder at the older man standing in the doorway to his mother's room. Griffen shook his head at Brandon, a silent warning to stay away. As the boys walked away, Griffen stepped backward into a nightmare.

The edge of the door barely missed clipping his nose as it slammed shut and locked him in the room with the possessed woman.

The stench of urine and feces wafted from Maddie's body. The cold mitigated some of the stench. Griffen tried briefly to imagine what it would smell like if this room were as hot as the rooms in the rest of the house. His carnival corn dog threatened to revisit him, so he pushed that thought out of his mind.

He returned his focus to Maddie as she stretched in unnatural ways. Her shoulder blades nearly touched as her arms reached behind her at an unseen object. As Griffen watched, her back arched as if she had sat up, but her head still pointed the opposite way. A gasp of pain escaped from deep inside Maddie as her legs folded under, then shot out in front of her. Her rear hung over the edge of the bed but at least her limbs, head, and chest aligned in the correct order. Maddie went limp, chin against chest, arms slack at her sides. Her breathing slowed and Griffen approached her. He could hear his footsteps on the brittle carpet and Maddie's kettle drum heartbeat.

"Maddie, it's Bishop Griffen. Are you well, Sister?" he asked, feeling stupid for asking a question he knew the answer to.

"We are hot, Elder," came the voice from her mouth. The slight accent was almost lost to Griffen beneath the sensation that Maddie spoke with more than one voice. Her own voice was the quietest.

"Is that why it's so cold in here? Because you're warm?"

"We burned in the lake. We burned in the shack where you saw us. We burn here," the voices said.

"I'm not speaking just to Maddie Smith, am I? Sister Madeline Smith, child of God, are you there?"

Her chin bounced up from her chest and she faced Griffen. Her eyes wide with fear and sweat pouring down her face, Maddie spoke. "Where are my boys, Bishop? Where are they?"

"They're here, but not in this room."

"We know where they are," said the other voices from Maddie's mouth. "We should invite them in to see their mother."

"No," Maddie screamed. "Leave them be."

"They'll not see you like this, Maddie. I know what is tormenting you and they know it. But I need help."

"Yesssssss," the voices said. "Su hermano. Sí, sí."

Her body twisted again so that she fully faced Griffen. He took a step toward her, hoping to help her lay down—on her back with all limbs pointed in the proper direction— when she began to rise from the bed. Her legs, hanging down, scraped up the bed as her thighs disconnected from the mattress. She rose until her head bumped the ceiling and her toes dangled above the bed.

"Bring us your brother in Christ and we shall see who tastes the flames of Hell today," Maddie—but not really Maddie—said. "Bring him and bring Him. We dare you. But leave us now and we shall have the flesh of her womb to feast on before your return."

"Leave my boys alone!" the real Maddie yelled, raising her arms and pushing against the ceiling. She collapsed into a heap of tested muscles, rolled onto her back, and appeared to sleep.

"Maddie?" Griffen whispered. "Heavenly Father, is she sleeping?"

A hand bolted out, grabbing Bishop Griffen at the elbow. "Get my sons out of here, but don't let them near that house, Bishop."

Her hand trailed away from him, and he knew…

***

"I knew that I had made a mistake I couldn't take back. I knew what house she meant because I had driven Brandon and David by it at Brandon's request before we went to the carnival. I took the photo and got out of there."

"Where are they now?" Montoya asked Griffen, shaking a bit at hearing his friend divulge an encounter with an evil he thought they'd been able to leave behind.

"I left them at Sister Christensen's house. I told them to go right up to the house as I wanted to get here as soon possible. I waited until the door opened."

"Back to your car, then. Unless you have any, we'll need to stop and get some consecrated oil. A lot of it."

"I knew coming here was right. I know we haven't talked about it, but I knew you'd not question what I have seen."

"'I am God and mine arm is not shortened and I will show miracles, signs, and wonders, unto all who believe in my name and whoso shall ask it in my name, in faith, they shall cast out Devils,'" Montoya said.

"Old Testament?" Griffen asked.

"Joseph Smith," Montoya answered. "We weren't the first to fight a demon."

"No, of course not. They are many, right?"

Montoya straightened his tie and put on his suitcoat, the armor of the Latter-day Saint. "Too many, and I want them out of our town and out of our lives for good."

"You aren't the only one."

"There are stories like ours. One about missionaries in California in the '60s—one of them might even have been from around here—feeling a presence at the home of a woman. They couldn't go past the fence to get into the house," Montoya said. "They pushed on and eventually saw the woman. According to what I heard, the woman had destroyed the inside of her home. When the missionaries calmed her down enough to talk, she told them that one of them would forsake the church and the other would be a lifelong member."

"This story come with any names?" Griffen asked.

"I don't recall exactly. Some Scandinavian name but not spelled like you'd think."

A picture from an obituary flashed in Griffen's mind: a recently departed friend from a nearby town, who served in Chico, California, about ten years before Griffen and Montoya served in South America. "Why is it always a woman? That one in California, ours in Santiago, Sister Smith now…" Griffen said.

"It's not always, but it seems to be that way more recently. Blame the movies, I guess. If Vera were still alive, she'd say it's because women are easier targets since they don't have priesthood power."

"Could be. That's not likely to change any time soon."

The two men prayed again before leaving Montoya's

home, thanking God for the ability to fight evil in His name through the authority of the priesthood granted to men in the church and praying to return to their homes soon.

***

Brandon tried to be fair to his little brother, so after asking Sister Christensen if he could go outside for some air, he whispered the truth to David.

"I don't think you should go there," David said quietly, but still louder than Brandon would have liked.

"I have to. Something happened to Mom there and that's why she's sick."

"Then I'm coming, too."

"No. If we both go, everyone will come for us instead of helping Mom. I'm just going to look around."

"And then you'll come right back?"

"I promise."

"I'm scared," the younger boy said, starting to shake. His body trembled and a folded-up piece of paper fell out of his pocket.

"I am, too, and that's why I gotta do this. For Mom." Brandon hugged his little brother, handed him the paper he'd dropped without looking at it, and kissed him on the head like he had seen their mother do countless times. "Stay cool, okay?"

"'K."

Brandon went out the front door, stretched and breathed deeply for a moment, then ran. He ran in the fading light of day with his head down, focused on his destination. Focused on saving his mother. He ran with such determination that he did not see his bishop and his stake president drive past him.

They didn't see him, either.

When he arrived at the corner home, it appeared black. The rooftop eclipsed the setting sun, covering the street and

Brandon in shadow. The windows were shuttered eyes and a dark hole had replaced the door. As he approached the porch, he saw that the darkness was not the door but rather what lay beyond it. The door stood open, not creaking on its hinges or propped with a doorstop. It held its place perpendicular to the frame, as if being held and inviting Brandon in.

He expected the door to slam shut behind him after he crossed the threshold. Instead, the door stayed in place as he shuffled through the first room and into the kitchen. When he looked back, the door had been closed without a sound.

Nothing, including Brandon, moved inside the house. He watched the door to see if it would open again. He watched for someone to have been behind the door or maybe a stray animal that could have pushed it closed. Through the windows, he saw trees sway in a breeze that hadn't been blowing before he entered the house and watched the dusk swallow the tops of those trees. After the long pause, Brandon lifted one foot and began walking again; whether anything walked with him, he couldn't say.

He now had two choices: he could go upstairs, where the dead-eyed windows lived, or he could go down into the cellar. Brandon thought of those windows and how far above the ground they were and decided to explore the lower level first.

Pushing the cellar door open with his foot, Brandon saved his hands to swat away any insects that might fly out at him. He pictured a swarm of gnats or midsummer wasps ready to sting him for invading their territory.

With the door open, Brandon inched his way forward and down onto the first step. It held his twelve-year-old weight without giving way and so he took the second step, letting the door shut softly behind him. Four steps down, Brandon's foot broke through a plank and he tumbled face first into the dirt floor.

Brandon landed in the dust and felt something harder

than the dirt beneath him. He stood, brushing the grime of the floor off himself as best he could, and noticed that he could see although he couldn't see a source of light in the room. He bent down to brush off the bottoms of his pantlegs and saw the shape of his body on the floor. His imprint seemed longer—taller if he'd been standing—than he felt himself to be. His hands farther from his feet than he thought they were. And then the ground rippled before his eyes. His sandy hands reached out for his real legs, the dirt thickening around bones.

He shuffled backward and the dirt that appeared to grow from the floor wafted back down. The bones of two hands protruded up from the surface.

***

After gathering all the consecrated oil and a sacrament tray with the two holy emblems they found at the stake center, Montoya and Griffen barreled their way to Maddie Smith's house. It struck Griffen how normal the daily rites of the Church were—the emblems of sacrament were tap water and white bread from one of the local grocery stores, the oil simple pure olive oil that had been set aside and consecrated just for the purpose of blessings and healings. Yes, both men were in suits, but that was no different from what they wore every day. Being summer, Griffen wore a short-sleeved button-up white shirt as he did so often in the humid mission field of Chile all those years before, but his dark blue tie hung the same no matter the length of his sleeves. He shared the same attitude Montoya had about the clean and well-pressed suit coats they wore: this was their armor against the world. And maybe Griffen's armor, the spiritual one only Heavenly Father could see had taken a few more dents than Montoya's, but here they were, together again and walking into a situation that as far as Griffen knew, few other men alive had faced before.

"Remember, Blaine," Montoya said, calling Griffen by

his given name for the first time in years, "we are not alone. What happened in Chile makes us the perfect vessels of God's will in this situation, even when we ourselves are not perfect."

Montoya could do that to Griffen better than anyone other than his wife had ever done. It scared him when Montoya moved to Blackhawk because Griffen was sure he would be a daily reminder of what they lost in the earthquake and the fires that followed. A reminder of his own weakness and inability to serve the Lord as fully as he desired. Instead, Montoya's presence as a friend and as someone rising through the ranks of Church hierarchy faster than himself helped Griffen through mistakes far worse than his failure in Chile. Only Montoya, Mrs. Griffen, and God knew Griffen's repentance and his journey back onto the straight and narrow path. He'd faced his own demons. Facing whatever had taken hold of Maddie Smith would be nothing more and nothing less than a service to Christ Jesus.

"This is it," Griffen said, pointing Montoya toward the Smith driveway. "Look, the door didn't even shut all the way behind me when I left."

"When the prophet Joseph Smith dispossessed Newel Knight, he did it just by touching his hand. If we are lucky, we'll not need to do more than that," Montoya said, pulling his suit coat tight around him and opening his door.

"If we'd known that in Santiago, maybe we wouldn't be here now."

"Perhaps, but she might still be, and then what? Some fresh-in-the-field elders, a year younger than we were, come here and don't have a clue what to do? Or someone else goes screaming to the Catholics in the old tabernacle downtown to bring in their Hollywood priests and make a spectacle of Sister Smith's ordeal? I won't have it. This is our home and we take care of our own."

As Montoya spoke, the scent of burning excrement

wafted toward the two men. Griffen expected it but still recoiled. Montoya turned into the bushes and vomited.

"Okay," Griffen said. "Sounds like you're ready." He clapped the other man on the back, offered him a handkerchief, and waited a moment. Once Montoya stood again, Griffen saw a resolve in his eyes he did not recognize.

"In the name of the Father, the Son, and the Holy Ghost, I hope you're right."

Chapter Nine: Choose the Right

Brandon stared at the bones, transfixed by the dirt of the floor that floated away from them. He thought of snow covering a barren field, but the opposite of that. The fingers of one hand pointed up and the other hand lay against the breastbone. A cord grew out from under that hand and at first Brandon thought it was a root that had twisted its way into the body. Somewhere nearby, he guessed, a tree fed and grew from the nutrients supplied by this hidden body. A closer looked revealed that the cord looped around the neck, the back of it now sunk into the vertebrae. The loop met again under the hand that had been against its chest for who knew how long.

He didn't want to touch it, but he knew he had to see what was under the bony hand and why it remained out of sight.

He knelt next the body, on the side opposite the arm he planned to move. Slowly, his own arm, not much shorter than the exposed arm near him, stretched out. His fingertips touched the hand and more silt drifted away. He pulled back a few inches; he expected the bones to be cold, but they were warm, almost hot.

Fresh, Brandon thought, but that couldn't be. There was nothing left but bones and the cord around the neck on this skeleton. Not a shred of clothing or muscle. Whoever

119

this was, they'd been here a long time. He took a deep breath, sucking in air that held particles of grave dirt, and grabbed the skeleton's right hand.

The hand didn't immediately give way and Brandon had to tug harder than he wanted to. He wanted to pull and let go. He yanked again and the hand flew away from its long-held spot. A circular object with a wide, flat side jumped in the air for a moment then fell back against the body's sternum. The cord—the necklace—was darker where it had been beneath the hand and two lines with a circle at the end had been imprinted on the breastbone and part of the ribs. The object that had been hanging from the end settled back into its accustomed place, flat side up. Brandon's eyes widened as he recognized what had been hidden.

He had one like it at home. His was thicker in the band and hadn't lost its shine like this one had. The flat side was a shield emblazoned with three letters: CTR.

Choose the Right.

He and every Mormon kid ever had that slogan pounded into them, especially when they turned eight and were baptized. His bishop at the time (not Bishop Griffen as bishops only served a few years before it was someone else's turn), had given him one that was made of a pliable metal. The green shield with the letters said something about who you were, he'd thought at the time. You went to church enough to be given a reminder of your commitment. Someone you knew and probably loved, baptized you and someone else, also someone you loved most likely, confirmed the Holy Ghost upon you. At eight years old, every LDS child with LDS parents did it. In towns like Blackhawk, you were weird if you didn't.

The CTR ring on this body wasn't like the first ring Brandon had had. Instead, it was like the one his mom gave him not long ago when he turned twelve and Bishop Griffen ordained him a deacon. The more substantial ring had been his grandfather's, worn when he served in the mission field in England. The green emblem and silver band served its own mission: that reminder not to stray, to stick to the straight and narrow path.

The owner of the ring Brandon looked at now had strayed. And at the final moments, either they or the person who had put them in this basement, decided to block out the reminder, to shut its green and gold away from view.

Reaching, sucking in more corpse dust and dirt, Brandon grasped the ring with a pincer grip. The cord snapped, a small *bang* in the cloistered basement. The ring nearly slipped out of his fingers, ready to roll around in the body's ribcage, forcing Brandon to reach in to get it or to leave it and pretend he never saw it.

After the quick slip, he held the ring tighter, bringing it closer to his eyes. He spun it through his fingers and noticed the inside of the band was not as smooth as the outside. Peering closer, he read the inscription to himself. Then he read it aloud to make sure he heard his own voice.

"Samantha Robinson 1991," Brandon first whispered then spoke louder to anything that might be in the basement with him. "Samantha Robinson 1991."

A scream built in his lungs and throat. He heard his mom screaming that name as her arms and legs swung wildly during the Mormon Miracle Pageant. And here, he guessed, was Samantha Robinson. What was left of her, anyway. The scream boiled in Brandon's pre-teen lungs again and he would have let it out, but a knocking above him caused Brandon to swallow the noise. He shut his mouth. Tears of fear poured down his cheeks. Teardrops darkened the dirt floor. Some landed on Samantha. Instead of bursting with noise, Brandon listened as best he could over the pounding of his heart.

***

The two men entered the home and marched straight through to the master bedroom. They paid no mind to the heat of the living room and did their best not to be beaten by the stench that radiated from their destination. Griffen raised his hand to knock but the door was already ajar. Montoya pushed it farther open.

Maddie lay on her bed, her breath quick and shallow, her eyes closed. Her left hand pointed toward the ceiling and her right hand lay between her breasts in a fist. Dark stains covered the nightgown she wore. The sheets and blankets formed a soft pile at the foot of the bed and the mattress appeared to sag and swell, like it was breathing but slower than Maddie's pace. When the mattress pulsed, a faint, brackish green light rippled out from it. The waves of light carried the fecal odor with it, but the stench was not as overpowering as it had been earlier.

Montoya walked around the bed, careful to avoid the pile of sheets and blankets and keeping an arm's length away from the mattress. He said nothing but kept his eyes on Maddie. Griffen kept his gaze on Montoya, watching for any signal or direction from his former mission companion. Ever since reuniting with Montoya when Montoya moved to Blackhawk, Griffen had felt the younger man was somehow older. Montoya held together better during the earthquake and even better under the scrutiny of the Church disciplinary council they faced afterward. Montoya, Griffen knew, forged ahead in his devotion to the Church and Heavenly Father. Griffen had wavered.

"Your faith let you down," came a voice from the bed. "And you let down your faith, Elder."

"To whom are we speaking?" Montoya asked, waving a hand to silence Griffen.

"To one who knows you well, Elder," said the voice. Both men stared at Maddie. She hadn't moved an inch, nor opened her eyes, but the voice came from her mouth.

"Not well enough," said Montoya. "We've been promoted a few times since our missions."

"Not high enough. I wish to see a higher authority than you dogs."

"The higher authority is always with us and even you are subject to it," Griffen said, speaking for the first time since entering the room.

"You'll burn the same. Just as this vessel will and as the one you failed does," said the voice. Maddie's face fought against a smile but lost to whatever moved her muscles. The twisted grin remained frozen in place, looking as if it would rip Maddie's face in two, then relented. The woman's mouth returned to a relaxed, neutral position, her lips throbbing slightly with her continued rapid breathing.

Griffen and Montoya moved toward each other, meeting at the foot of the bed. Griffen was about to speak, but Montoya cut him off.

"Whatever it is, it knows something, but not everything. It doesn't know, or won't acknowledge, your repentance. Don't let it bait you."

"Rey, I…" Griffen started. He stood upright, straightened his coat and tie, and put his hands on Montoya's shoulders. "I'm good. The Lord is our shepherd and He will see us through this."

Laughter emanated from the area around Maddie's head. Not so much from her mouth but from the air around her. Her breathing stopped, the mattress ceased pulsating, and all the light—natural, unnatural, or supernatural—went out.

***

The knocking stopped and was followed by footsteps. Brandon did his best to follow the steps, but he couldn't tell if only one person entered the house or if more walked the floor above him. The steps started and stopped and soon Brandon heard voices. The steps and the voices moved away from each other, confirming the presence of at least two people. Brandon's eyes glanced at the painting on the far wall and saw that the men in the painting had changed places. One stood closer to the woman while the other two were now positioned nearer the corners of the scene. Above him, the voices came from a similar triangular pattern, one after another.

"We know someone is here," came the first voice.

"We'll find you," said the second, higher pitched voice.

"Nowhere to hide," a third voice, the calmest of the three said.

Would they stick together to search the house?, Brandon wondered. Or would they split up, each taking a level? They were right, he didn't have anywhere to hide. For now, he scooted beneath the stairs, just in case one came down to the cellar. He closed his eyes and listened.

***

The darkness enveloped Montoya and Griffen. The putrid odors thickened, leaving moisture on their bodies like handprints from a child who'd been playing in mud. The wetness burned on Griffen but chilled Montoya. Griffen moved away from Montoya, first keeping a hand on his companion's shoulder, then separating from him to move to the other side of Maddie. Her breathing quickened and grew louder, helping the men keep her located.

"Can you hold her head while I pour the oil on her?" Montoya asked.

Griffen nodded, then said, "Yes." He reached out, following the sounds of Maddie's breath. The air escaping her mouth hit Griffen's hands with a burst of thick, vomitous radiation. He placed one hand beneath her head and the other on her forehead. She didn't struggle.

Dribbling the consecrated oil on her head, Montoya asked, "What is her full name?"

"Madeline Patricia Smith," Griffen responded.

"Married?"

"Divorced."

"What is her maiden name?"

"Give me a second, it'll come to me."

"Use it when we do the second blessing. I'll do the anointing," Montoya said as he placed his hands, palms down, on the top of Maddie's head.

"Madeline Patricia Smith, by the power of the Melchizedek Priesthood which we hold, we anoint this consecrated oil upon your head for the purpose of healing. We do this in the name of Jesus Christ. Amen."

Griffen repeated the agreement, still holding Maddie's head tight. Their eyes had grown accustomed to the dark enough to see Maddie start to move. Beneath Griffen's hands, her head remained still. The rest of her body began to convulse and twist. Her knees bent up to her chest and shot back out, threatening to pull her head out of Griffen's grip. Then her shoulders and arms contorted, first rolling as if Maddie simply wanted to turn over while sleeping, but not stopping. The sounds of bones cracking and likely breaking rang out as Maddie's back became visible to both men. The nightgown she wore had been shredded. Red lash marks covered her back. Blood pulsed from the lashes but then appeared to be sucked back into her body. She continued to roll until her chest again faced the ceiling, her breathing slowed, and her breasts rose and fell.

Griffen never let go of her head. Maddie didn't make a sound, other than her breathing.

"Dear Lord," Griffen said. "How could she live through that?"

"Joseph Smith wrote that when he saw Newel Knight, the man's face and body were twisted into all sorts of shapes," Montoya said.

"Knight," Griffen shouted. "That's Maddie's maiden name."

A laugh roiled from between Maddie's lips. A deep sound, without a speck of humor.

"She came to me and now she's mine," said a voice all too familiar to Montoya and Griffen. "What escaped before has returned to me."

"Do the blessing now, Blaine!" Montoya said. Griffen released his grip on Maddie's head and placed his hands next to Montoya's at the crown of her head.

"Madeline Patricia Knight Smith," Griffen began, speaking over the laugh that continued to emanate from the woman on the bed, "By the power of the Melchizedek Priesthood which we hold, we seal the anointing of oil and —"

The room exploded with light, first a green and red, sickly light from the bed. Then the diseased glow was swallowed by a white-yellow light from above. The clean light pushed the dusky hue downward and for a moment Maddie appeared radiant, even healthy. A dark cloud hovered over her body and soon sank back into her as the light pushed down. Soon the room was dark again. Maddie lay still, her breathing barely perceptible.

"Finish the blessing," Montoya said.

***

The door atop the stairs shook then slammed open. Dust fell on Brandon as someone descended the stairs under which he hid.

"Dammit," the high-pitched voice squealed. "Damn, damn, damn." Footsteps pounded down the steps, missing the broken bottom two. Brandon opened his eyes and saw just feet and legs: slender, muscular legs in tight jeans. There was a word for these jeans that he'd heard from his mom, but he couldn't remember it. They looked like the time Brandon had knocked over a bottle of bleach while Maddie was cleaning, and it spilled on her dark blue slacks. The feet were clad in boots with a thick, yellowish rubber sole. The feet came to a stop where Brandon had recently been, next to the exposed skeleton of Samantha Robinson.

"Doug," the man yelled, "someone's been down here. Someone found the girl."

Another set of feet came down the stairs, but much slower. They stopped next to the first man and then Brandon heard that third, calmer voice.

"She's still here and there aren't a bunch of cops outside, which means whoever found her is still in the house. Ill check the cellar. You go back upstairs with Marlon and finish looking through the first floor then head to the top. Keep quiet until you find someone, or you know things are clear. And Randy, don't be screaming."

"Yeah, Doug. Fine."

Randy, owner of the high-pitched voice and bleached jeans, went back upstairs, passing above Brandon but never seeing him.

Brandon's eyes tried to focus on the remaining man— Doug—but his gaze drifted again to the demonic painting. It had changed again, become clearer. The man next to the woman wore dark pants and boots, a leather jacket covering the chest and back. Brandon looked at Doug and saw the same clothes. Looking back at the painting, he saw the boots and splotchy jeans of Randy on one man, a work shirt, like a mechanic would wear, covered his top. And although Brandon couldn't tell for sure, he guessed that the name patch on the front read "Randy." In the painting, the third man also wore boots and black pants. He wore a long, black coat, something Brandon remembered his dad calling a duster. *Cowboys used to wear them and guys who ride motorcycle sometime do,* his dad had said. *Usually dudes with something else to hide.*

Brandon didn't want to meet Marlon and whatever he had to hide, but he also didn't want Doug to find him. As Brandon contemplated an escape route, Doug walked away from the skeleton in the dirt floor toward the painting on the wall. He touched it with his fingertips and all the colors swirled together. When the swirling ended, the frame filled with the face of the devil and one red, black-tipped finger pointing out, pointing right at Brandon.

As Doug turned around, Brandon covered his mouth to stifle a scream. He tried to pull his body into itself, to take up as little space as possible, hoping not to be seen. Doug stepped over Samantha Robinson, still in the middle of the floor, still dead, and was almost to the stairs when banging from above stole his focus.

"Ow, Marlon, you shithead," Brandon heard Randy say. "That fucking hurt."

"You assholes," Doug said, and leapt up the stairs. "What the fuck is going on?"

In another situation, Brandon would have let himself be shocked at hearing the F-word. He'd been grounded once when Maddie heard him listening to a song that had the word in it. Now, though, more pressing matters needed attention. With Doug upstairs again, he could get away. He could find something to stand on and break one of the painted-over windows and crawl through it. He could wait, hoping the three men would go to the top level of the house, leaving the front door wide open. He could...

He could only stare at the painting, still filled with the image of the devil. The finger that a moment ago pointed at him now curled to beckon him. He walked toward it, one hand reaching out, the other against his side, clutching Samantha Robinson's CTR ring in a tight fist. He felt pulled toward the painting, even as it changed before his eyes. The devil, all red and veiny muscles, shrank to show the house they were in and another familiar place: his house. Another step closer and the houses were replaced by rooms. In one corner, Brandon saw the very basement he was in and three men—Doug, Randy, and Marlon—alone in a circle, then with a young woman in the circle, laying on her back, a knife protruding from her chest. In the other corner, his house morphed into his mother's bedroom. At first, Maddie was alone. Then another body appeared, floating above her as she lay on her bed. Next, the amorphous body dispersed, and two men were in the room with Maddie. One was Bishop Griffen. The other Brandon recognized but couldn't name.

Just for a moment, he saw his own bedroom, David sitting on the floor, turning a sheet of paper over and over without reading it.

The images of his house soon became washed out with a brilliant white light so bright Brandon had to look away, back to the other room. There, he saw himself from behind, staring at the painting. Then, the painted image of himself was no longer alone.

Chapter Ten: And Should We Die

Bishop Griffen breathed deeply, despite the foul stench looming in the air. The air thickened in his mouth and his throat tightened. He tried taking another breath but instead swallowed an invisible pudding that clogged his lungs, making further breathing feel impossible.

"Finish the blessing, Bishop," Montoya said, not taking his hands away from Maddie. "Finish or we will have to start over."

Swallowing hard, Griffen opened his mouth to continue the blessing over Maddie. In his head, he heard the words, but a chirping sound, cricket-like—spouted from his lips instead. He swallowed again, but the chirping continued. He coughed and felt tiny legs in his throat and insectile wings against his inner cheek. Another cough and a swarm of black Mormon crickets flew out of his mouth and onto Maddie, covering her face and the hands of the two men.

The crickets scrambled over Maddies's face, tickling Griffen's hands with tiny feet and wings. He could feel the probing jaws of the crickets searching for food that didn't exist.

With nothing else to feed on, the insects began devouring each other. The larger crickets ate the smaller and then each other until one improbably-sized red-bellied cricket remained. It fluttered its wings and snuffled Maddie's neck and upper chest, then her chin before appearing to focus on her lips. Maddie opened her mouth and bit through it, spraying its juices and bits of undigested crickets down her chin and over her chest. Griffen gagged at the sight but found his lungs and throat clear again.

"Madeline Patricia Knight Smith, in the name of our Savior Jesus Christ and by the power of the Melchizedek Priesthood which we hold, we seal the anointing oil upon you and bless you that you may be rid of this affliction. Whether earthly sickness or demonic ailment, we bless you in Christ to be healed, and remind you that repentance is always available to you, you child of God. Thy will be done, Lord, for Sister Smith, as it was fulfilled when Thy son bled for our sins and rose again. Thou hast beaten Satan himself and given we your servants the power to do so in Thy name. Like Thine prophet on Earth before us, we cast this nameless demon out from Thy child and bless her and call her to any repentance she may need.

"We say this in the name of Jesus Christ. Amen."

"Amen," Montoya echoed.

Neither man removed his hands from Maddie's head, covered in filth and sweat as they were. Beneath them, Maddie didn't stir, didn't open her mouth again, or move to wipe the entrails and remains of the oversized Mormon cricket from her face. Then she coughed and both men recoiled, expecting vomit at the least and only God knew what at the worst. She sat up, the tendons of her hips and back cracking as she did. She coughed again, as if ready to speak. She turned her head, her neck grinding against itself, two loose plates clattering against each other after her body had spun completely around, and glanced casually at Griffen first, then turned to Montoya.

"You know what he did? When you left that festering southern country?" came the words from Maddie's mouth, but not in her voice. The speaker's accent was more like

Montoya's maternal grandmother, a descendant of indigenous peoples whom some of his fellow Mormons have tried to tell him were the Nephites of the Book of Mormon. "Do you know what your friend did?"

"Bishop Griffen's transgressions were forgiven, as are all the sins of those who repent to Christ. Were you there? When Christ our Lord visited Hell before He was resurrected?" Montoya said, straightening his sleeves.

She smirked and spat at Montoya. A glob of cricket guts hit his lapel and slowly dripped off. The lights of the room flashed again and somewhere in the house a bulb exploded. "We are many and all were there...from the beginning."

"You belong back in the fire," Griffen screamed and raised a hand, ready to strike Maddie, hoping to hurt whatever was inside her.

Montoya caught Griffen's eyes and held them. The old sin passed in silence—the drinking, the fight Griffen had with his first fiancé, the car accident that thankfully hurt no one more than Griffen himself—and Griffen lowered his hand.

"It wants you to lash out," Montoya said. "Anger is its weapon, not ours."

"Rey, I just..." Griffen paused and broke eye contact with Montoya. He turned his gaze on Maddie and tried to look beyond the face that stared back. Weekly, he renewed his covenant with Heavenly Father, as they would by ministering the sacrament to Maddie had they not left the emblems in the car. "I am right with the Lord. My sin is in not doing enough to serve others. I have too long ignored the ills of others who are like I was. Heavenly Father, forgive me for being a poor servant."

"He does," Montoya said. "Now let's finish this."

Shaking the bottle of consecrated oil over Maddie's head again, Montoya lifted his chin toward Griffen and motioned for their hands to be placed over the oil again.

Maddie screamed as oil touched her scalp, but didn't lie back down. She flailed her arms out, punching and grasping, searching for anything to grab hold of. The men avoided her clawing fingers, her nails brushing their suit coats but not getting even a pinch of fabric.

"Anoint, seal, bless," Montoya said under his breath, then repeated it louder. "Anoint, seal, bless!"

"Let's end this now," Griffen said, placing his hands upon Maddie's head.

"Madeline Patricia Knight Smith," Montoya began, "by the power of the Melchizedek Priesthood bestowed upon us by the spirit of the living God, we anoint this consecrated oil upon you for the purpose of healing your spirit and body. In the name of Jesus Christ, amen."

"Amen," Griffen said.

A mix of screaming and laughing emanated from Maddie, but the men continued.

"Madeline Patricia Knight Smith, we seal this anointing by the laying on of hands upon you with the power of the Melchizedek Priesthood which we hold. Maddie, in the name of Jesus Christ, the only begotten Son of our Father in Heaven, we command the demonic influence inside you to leave. We command the bodiless, nameless spirit to get behind thee and leave our presence. We command in the name of Jesus that this fallen angel, who lost the war in Heaven in the pre-existence, be cast back down into the fire it rose from. We—"

"I have a name and I shall not be mocked!" Maddie growled.

"By the power of the Holy Ghost, we demand your name," Montoya said.

"I am Ruin and so you shall be," the demon said.

"So be it," Griffen said, then resumed the blessing over Maddie. "Ruin, we command in Christ that you leave this vessel and return to the fire of Hell. We bless Maddie, we bless her physical body, her spiritual body, and her mind, that she may be rid of you. This we do in the name of Jesus Christ. Amen."

Tendrils of smoke curled Maddie's hair through the hands of the men blessing her. Their palms began to burn but they did not lift them from her.

"Ruin, if that is your name, we who hold Priesthood power from God the Father, His Son Jesus Christ, and the Holy Ghost, propel you back into the fires of Hell in which you shall burn until Judgment Day when we shall all kneel before Christ. In his name, Amen," Montoya said.

"Amen," Griffen said.

"Nema," Maddie said, accentuating the *A* in parody of the prayer ending. "We shall all burn together in Satan's house, be it this one … or another."

"The Lord has said He hath many houses," Montoya said. "Which do you mean?"

"This house," Maddie said as more smoke drifted from her body. "Or another. We shall all burn with it."

A cloud of acrid smoke, tinged with ash, poured out of Maddie's mouth and nose. The cloud congealed, sucking up the filth of the room and forming a misshapen body. Maddie fell back onto the bed, leaving Griffen's and Montoya's hands hanging in the air. The smoke-body hovered above them and where a mouth might have been, an endlessly black hole formed. What should have been lips moved and a tongue of flame flicked out. The cloud smacked its smoggy lips and spoke.

"We shall burn together, if not here, then another house we shall leave in ruin, in my name. The matches of Lucifer are now being lit by the knight's kin."

"Oh, Lord, no," Griffen said, stumbling around the bed and out of the bedroom. "Stay with her, Rey. Brandon…"

"Brandon?" Maddie muttered, weak but in her own voice. "Is he here? Please don't let him see me like this."

"Stay here," Griffen called back. "I'll get your boys."

Part Three:
Massacre

But if I with the finger of God cast out devils, no doubt the kingdom of God has come upon you.
—Luke 11:20, King James Bible

Chapter Eleven: Until the Wicked are Stubble

The painting changed. The colors shifted behind the crimson-skinned Devil and Brandon saw his mother, sitting up in bed and surround by grasshoppers. Then she was gone, the painting rippled, and Brandon saw himself. Not his face, like he would have when looking into a mirror, but his back. His dust-covered shoulders, his right hand a fist around an object he'd almost forgotten, and the floor of the cellar behind him. Where Samantha Robinson's body was in the real room, there was a circle drawn on the floor and surrounded by candles. Then the circle disappeared as a black boot crossed the line and stepped hard in the center. The body above the boot neared the Brandon in the painting, a hand reached out to take hold of Brandon. He turned before the hand could fall and…

He remained alone in the room. He saw shadows of feet in the crack of the door at the top of the stairs. Three voices spoke, Doug telling Marlon to stay in the kitchen to watch the cellar door and directing Randy toward the front door, just in case. "Whoever is down there, don't let him sneak by. He can't get out of here."

The two men took their orders silently and the door began to open. Brandon took one last glance at the painting, but it was black. He touched it to be sure it was real and wished he hadn't. The dirty air around him seemed to sigh in relief. The tip of his finger stung, then itched, then burned. He drew it toward his mouth, but paused as the finger turned red, then black, then back to its normal pale tone. The door above his head paused in its track but now continued to open.

Frozen to his spot, Brandon wanted to yell, to plead, but he felt a crawling contentment come over him. The feeling started in his finger, he noticed. He could do nothing but await his fate.

He looked behind him and saw the painting rearrange again. The cellar room returned, this time with the exposed skeleton of Samantha Robinson in the center, mere inches from where Brandon stood. But he was not in the painting. He turned hurriedly toward the stairs and the now open door atop it. Doug no longer obfuscated by the stairs or vaguely represented in paint stared right at Brandon as he descended the rickety steps.

Be still.

Brandon heard the words as if spoken directly in his ear. He'd spent his life being told to listen for the still, small voice of the Holy Ghost, the Spirit of the Lord who would guide him during troubled times. He listened, but nothing felt holy about this voice.

Still.

Having nowhere to go, Brandon stood still. Doug crept to the cellar floor, glancing at the skeleton, gazing at the painting, not seeing Brandon. With his heavy black boot, Doug kicked dirt over Samantha's remains, then knelt and picked up her hand.

"You've been here a long time, girl," he said. "You see anyone down here lately? That other woman, yeah, we know. Anyone else?"

Samantha said nothing. The voice, for good or ill, told Brandon to walk.

Circling Samantha's corpse in the opposite direction from Doug, Brandon took one step closer to the stairs. He didn't dare look back, fearing this invisibility would end if he did.

Another step.

Another.

The voice did not speak but he felt its prompting, its reminder to not run but take deliberate steps toward the stairs and an escape from this cellar tomb. Behind Brandon, Doug shuffled around, looking in all the nooks and crannies of the cellar. As Brandon placed his foot on the first step, he saw Doug bending beneath the stairs where Brandon had hidden earlier. A silver rectangle fell out of Doug's pocket and bounced close to Brandon.

Pick it up.

Brandon didn't know anyone who smoked, but he knew a lighter when he saw one. He picked it up with his left hand, Samantha's CTR ring still clutched in his right. With the two objects in hand, Brandon plodded his way up the stairs, carefully stepping over the broken landings. Beneath him, Doug cursed more, words Brandon had never heard. He wanted out and wished he'd never come here. He didn't have any answers about what happened to his mom, but he was certain that Doug, Marlon, and Randy had killed and buried Samantha Robinson. He had to get out before they killed him, too.

"Marlon," Doug yelled, causing Brandon to trip into the door and close it. "Marlon, you see anyone?"

"Nah. You? You right there closing the door?" Marlon said.

"No, dammit. Open it!"

Brandon moved so that the swinging door would miss him. He looked straight into Marlon's face and had to squeeze to not wet himself. A scar ran across Marlon's forehead and one eye yellowed with disease. He snarled, showing a gap of missing teeth and others nearly rotted away. He filled the door frame with aged muscle. Any hope of escape left Brandon.

I have made a way.

Marlon took a step backward, as if being gently pushed and his foot hit something on the floor. The small can clunked as it tipped, its red plastic lid falling off, causing clear liquid to splash onto Marlon's pants and the floor.

Use the lighter.

The silver rectangle weighed his hand down, but Brandon opened his fist, flicked the top off, and wondered exactly how to make the lighter work.

Do it now.

"I don't know how," he whispered, afraid the man before him would hear, even if he couldn't see.

Do it.

An image came into Brandon's head. His thumb on the ridged wheel of the lighter, pulling down on the wheel, a flame popping out from the top. Without thinking about it, Brandon performed the same action while seeing it happen in his head. He didn't see what he did next, either in is mind's eye or for real.

He'd closed his eyes as the flames engulfed Marlon's legs and spread across the floor. The ancient linoleum curled under the fire and the fire did not take long to lick the wooden frame of the cellar door. Marlon screamed, dropping to the floor and covering himself with more fire, not stamping it out as Brandon had learned to do. Brandon was able to jump over the large man as Marlon tumbled down the cellar stairs and into Doug, lighting the frail steps as he fell. Hearing the screams, Randy rushed to the kitchen and right into the fire. He tripped, nearly plowing into Brandon, and slid through the growing flames and right into the cellar with his friends.

Brandon looked back, saw the three men piled on each

other over the remains of Samantha Robinson, fire eating away their clothes and skin. On the far wall, the devilish painting melted, but not before Brandon saw the smiling face of Satan, redder than the fire, the smile meant just for him. Brandon couldn't look away, even as fire he'd been spared from tickled his feet, wanting to swallow him, too.

Stay with me.

Yes, he thought. I'll stay. It's warm, I won't be alone. I won't have to worry about Mom or David. Mom!

He tore his eyes away from the painting, not seeing the movement below him. As he began to walk—no, run!—his pants snagged on something.

Doug had climbed the steps and grabbed Brandon's ankle. Brandon kicked out, causing him to fall into the fire. Doug pulled and Brandon searched for anything to grab to hoist himself away or to strike Doug and earn his release.

"You little son of a bitch," Doug said, his face framed in the fire consuming him. "You belong here."

"Watch your language," said a new voice, a real voice, not one inside Brandon's head.

Bishop Griffen grabbed Brandon under his armpits and ripped him from Doug's grip. Griffen stood Brandon up, held the hand that started the fire, and they ran for the front door. Doug continued cursing but Brandon couldn't hear the words over the roaring of the growing fire. Decrepit wallpaper curled around them as they headed for the door. Scraps lighted their shoulders, but no flame took hold.

The front door stood open and only the bare but burning living room floor blocked their path. They crossed the floor carefully, watching the fire from the cellar meet the fire from the kitchen. The one hundred-fifty-year-old hardwood floor creaked and groaned, the weight of decades easing the fire's ability to destroy it.

The young man and the old man quickened their pace. Halfway across the floor, a board broke beneath Griffen and his leg shot through it. Tripping, Griffen pushed Brandon toward the open door. He fell and for a moment the floor held.

And then it could hold no longer.

"Bishop!" Brandon lunged toward the hole in the floor, but was too late. He peered into the growing chasm but saw only fire. The flames scorched his hair as he looked for any sign of life. From above, pieces of the ceiling fell into the hole and any chance that Bishop Griffen survived were gone.

Outside, out of the cellar, out of the house of the devil, Brandon sat on the lawn, watching the emergency lights approach, and cried.

Chapter Twelve: Serpents and Scorpions

His hands lay flat against a cool white sheet and he was sure he'd lost Samantha's CTR ring. Did he drop it leaping for Bishop Griffen? Yes, that must have been it. He wanted to cry at the loss and remembered bigger things than a ring had been lost. He heard voices, sometimes his name, other names, Bishop Griffen's name…

One voice made him open his eyes. His mother. "Mom," he said, struggling to say the word. The skin around his mouth felt tight, like he'd been sunburnt. His entire face pulled against itself and he remembered looking into the fire for Bishop Griffen. Trying again, the word came out clearer. "Mom!"

"Honey, I'm here," Maddie said. She held one of his hands, the right hand still missing the ring. "Mommy's here."

Brandon painfully opened his eyes. His mom looked like a disheveled angel, her hair wild, her clothes rumpled, but her eyes sparkled for the first time in months. "Mom," Brandon said. "I'm sorry. I'm so sorry." She wrapped her arms around him, and he didn't let himself even sigh as her arms grazed his sore body, the patches of burnt skin aching the most.

"Brandon, son, don't be. You're okay. I'm okay. David

is okay."

"But…but Bishop Griffen isn't. He's…he fell and he…"

"He saved you from that fire and he helped save me from … something else."

"I saw him, Mom. Not the Bishop. I saw *him*. He was in a painting and…"

Maddie squeezed Brandon and he couldn't hold back his cries any longer. He gasped as her arms tightened around him. "Did you touch it? Please, Jesus, tell me you didn't."

"I…it burned up, Mom. I saw it burn."

"Good, sweetie, good. I'm glad it's gone."

Brandon's eyes slipped shut again. "Can I rest a bit more?"

"Yes," Maddie said, knowing the next few days could be even worse for her son.

***

Stake President Rey Montoya sat in his office at the Nebo stake center, a Latter-day Saint chapel like so many others. A few doors down, a ward member emptied the baptismal font and would fill it again with clean, lukewarm water.

We aren't supposed to be lukewarm, Montoya thought. The undecided have decided to serve evil.

Rey had said as much hours earlier at the funeral of his long-time friend, Blaine Griffen. Blaine, even in his transgression, never turned lukewarm. What Rey wanted to say but couldn't was that Blaine had been through the fires for his love of Christ. But no, no, he couldn't tell anyone what had happened in Chile or why Blaine had gone into that house and not come out. He had stood at the pulpit scant feet away from the remains of his friend and could only say that remaining faithful through trials and loving those in need —as Blaine had done—forged the path to God's glory. He believed, he told those in attendance, in Jesus Christ and he believed that he would see his friend, perfected by the resurrection, again.

He shook many hands, often using the two-handed style he's once heard jokingly called the Bishop's grip. Most of those hands were members of the ward Griffen served as bishop, others from the wards in the Nebo stake. Briefly, he thought he saw someone who looked like Mitt Romney, but the lack of a security detail nixed that thought. He did not see Maddie Smith or her sons.

Now, alone with a cooling dish of leftover funeral potatoes, Montoya spread two documents across his desk. The first, only a few days old, was a copy of the *The Daily Herald* from nearby Provo showing a photo of the house in Blackhawk still aflame. Below it were headshots of Griffen and Samantha Robinson. The other three men found in the cellar had been identified but their names were not being released. The article stated they were now suspects in the murder of Samantha Robinson. Furthermore, a 12-year-old boy had escaped the fire, sustaining minor injuries.

The second document wasn't that old, either, although the information it contained was from 1977. Provided by Taysom the archivist, the document detailed the account of two missionaries in Toronto who attempted to dispossess a woman who could predict the future via demonic powers. New Testament tales swirled in Montoya's head as he read the pages. The young men—the same ages Griffen and Montoya had been when they were in Chile—were unsuccessful. The demonic presence asked to combat the highest official of the church and was rewarded by confronting the local mission president.

Montoya stopped reading. All this was too familiar. But somewhere there must be a clue to knowing if this was over, this time.

Continuing, Montoya read the name of the mission president: M. Russell Ballard. Ballard, he knew, was now the president of the church's Quorum of the Twelve, the Latter-day Saint equivalent to Jesus Christ's twelve apostles, and one step down from the three-member First Presidency. Further, the account claimed that Ballard was able to complete the dispossession after the failure of a Stake President, not because of lack of Priesthood power, but because of "Satan's respect for hierarchical bureaucracy."

Laughing, Montoya hoped that the presence calling itself Ruin respected his authority enough to be banished. He jotted a note to call Taysom and seek his opinion on how to relate the recent occurrences to his area president, who could very well take the tale to President Ballard himself. Not reporting the incident with Maggie Smith and how Griffen came to be in that house never crossed his mind as an option, but how to do it?

A scoop of potatoes went into his mouth and although they were cold, he chewed and swallowed. A yellow legal pad sat next to the papers he had been reading. Montoya took the pad and began to write, addressing his notes to Taysom.

I served the Lord and His one true church as a missionary in Santiago, Chile, in 1973 and '74. My companion Blaine Griffen and I lost four of our brothers and our mission president in a fire that followed an earthquake, as if we were like the prophet Elijah and unable to hear the Spirit. We also lost a young woman in the fire and I fear that she still burns in the fires of Hell because we could not save her.

We promised to tell no man what happened there, as Jesus directed his disciples to do after healing a man afflicted with demons.

You asked, Taysom, what my interest was in dispossessions. I am breaking my promise now so that you may know.

The pages of the pad turned quickly, filling with words in Montoya's flowing script. By the end, his hand ached, his heart raced, and his spirit soared.

Lawrence Welk on PBS and a cold can of Sprite awaited him at home.

***

At home, Maddie had cleaned up before bringing Brandon back. She'd cleaned out the fridge and restocked with her last approved trip to the Bishop's Storehouse. She swept, scrubbed, vacuumed, and washed and folded laundry. The cleanse was as much for her as her sons. The sisters did the best they could, but no one could clean a house like the homeowner, Maddie thought. Her room had been the worst. The sheets—she couldn't afford to, really—she threw away. She'd intended to wash them, but when she pulled them off her bed, a dark red cricket had leapt out at her and she knew the end had come for that set.

Focusing on Brandon and cleaning helped to keep her mind off how sick she had been. Mail had piled—none with the dreaded bold red letters on them, thank you—and her ancient answering machine had filled up. The phone messages were the worst. Messages from the cherry plant, first wishing her well, then asking when she might return to her shift, and then informing her that her position had been filled for the rest of the summer. That would be okay. One of the letters had been her teaching contract renewal, which she signed and returned to the school district office in person. No one in the office said anything about her being sick or even questioned her contract status. She watched an administrative assistant stamp the contract **APPROVED** and she left the building smiling.

Later, while picking up some ice cream, she heard someone say something about a woman who freaked out at the Mormon Miracle Pageant. Briefly, Maddie thought the speaker was pointing at her, but as far as she remembered her trip to the pageant had been the last pleasant thing she did before falling ill.

Gossips will gossip, she thought. *I hope they can repent and be clear of that with their bishops.*

Then she thought of Bishop Griffen and wished

Brandon had been well enough to attend the funeral.

***

The doctor told him not to scratch no matter how much he itched.

"You'll peel the bandages away from the healing skin," the doctor said. "It's not going to be fun, but you got out lucky. No third-degree burns. Your mom will help you apply the salve and you'll be fine soon. No swimming, though."

Brandon had nodded through all of that, mostly listening. Now, home at last, all he wanted to do was scratch. He couldn't remember having chicken pox, but listening to his mom, he must have wanted to scratch all over back when he was two. She showed him a photo of himself sitting in the bath, red dots covering his small body, Maddie dumping water over him, his hands wrapped in fabric. His mom being in the picture meant his dad must have taken it.

If Dad hadn't left, none of this would have happened, Brandon thought. He felt a patch of skin on his arm tighten, then loosen, as if something crawled up his arm. The sensation slithered up his arm and spread across his chest. If only he could scratch.

Eyes closed, Brandon tried to ignore the itching, the healing skin, and think instead about something good. Nothing came to him. That, however, was better than one of the alternatives. At night, when he closed his eyes, he saw two things: Bishop Griffen falling through the floor, burning to death and the red, grinning face of the devil in the painting. If he kept his eyes closed long enough, the devil's face turned into his own. His black-tipped finger would stretch out, pointing at Brandon, then at something behind him. If he turned, he'd wake up, rustling his bandages and sighing in pain. David, thankfully, slept on the couch in the living room for the first few days after Brandon returned home. Otherwise, he was sure he'd have kept his little brother awake all night.

At times, the itching ceased. Brandon lay still in his bed, saying prayers of thankfulness for the relief. He could not pray for long, though.

"Dear Heavenly Father. I thank Thee for bringing me home and for healing my mom. Lord, please be with her and with Bishop Griffen's family. Let them know I am sorry for what happened. I say this in the name of Jesus Christ… Amen."

Stings pierced his body when he closed his prayers. Small, but sharp and painful. He had to take huge breaths before saying *amen*. He checked to see if something was indeed stinging him the first time, but saw nothing but his own red and blistered skin. When sleep came, it came in tumultuous waves. Fires, red faces, failed prayers, and a desire to be held and left alone at the same time. Sleep felt as dangerous as being awake.

Sunday, he knew, he would volunteer to serve the sacrament. He'd feel better if he did. And then, soon, this summer would be behind his family and him. Things could be normal again. Things could be just like they were.

That night he dreamt of a man who looked like his grandfather leading a band of pink-suited men playing music Brandon had never heard. Near them, another man of the same age watched the band and drank a soda. The man glanced over his shoulder and mouthed a word Brandon couldn't hear. The band played as a bubble machine whirred to life. Glimmering bubbles soon obscured the band and the man watching, leaving a tinted darkness behind.

Chapter Thirteen: Families are Forever

President Rey Montoya presided over the Blackhawk Third Ward's August Fast and Testimony meeting. The first Sunday of every month, the LDS faithful were directed to fast for two meals and then offer the money they would have spent for food to the church in addition to their usual ten percent tithe. Fast offerings were like an extra jolt of faith to start the month. This Sunday, the ward could use all the extra faith they could get.

Montoya sat in the same cushioned seat nearest the pulpit he'd inhabited during Griffen's funeral, the ward's choir behind him, and did his best to project strength to the congregation that had lost its leader. Soon enough, a new bishop—and a new bishopric as each bishop is direct by the spirit to choose his councilors—would be set apart and ordained from members of the very congregation seated before him. Although the church's Articles of Faith declare a belief in pastors, teachers, and evangelists, it is strictly organizational. Being the bishop does not mean you are the one standing before the congregation week by week preaching a sermon. Fast and Testimony meeting served as a good example of that.

After opening prayers and the passing of the sacrament, members were invited to step up to the pulpit and bear their testimonies. Sometimes children would speak, their parents whispering a testimony in the child's ear. Having not grown up in the church, this always rankled Montoya, but he said nothing. He hoped today would be filled with the spirit of the Lord amid pain and suffering and less self-righteous parading of children.

First, though, the meeting had to open. He concentrated on the upcoming sacrament and the words of the accompanying prayers.

"O God, the Eternal Father, we ask thee in the name of thy Son, Jesus Christ, to bless and sanctify this bread to the souls of all those who partake of it; that they may eat in remembrance of the body of thy Son, and witness unto thee, O God, the Eternal Father, that they are willing to take upon them the name of thy Son, and always remember him, and keep his commandments which he has given them, that they may always have his Spirit to be with them. Amen."

As the young priest intoned the blessing, an odor wafted to Montoya's nose. He looked up, knowing that no one else would be able—the congregation with heads bowed and arms folded—to pinpoint the source. The smell emanated from near the deacons, praying before standing to receive their trays of bread to pass among the congregation. With their heads bowed, Montoya couldn't identify the deacons by their faces, but the bandages poking out from the collar of one boy were unmistakable: Brandon Smith.

The prayer ended, the deacons stood and waited in turn. Brandon took his tray. He walked to the back of the congregation where fewer pews were occupied. Montoya watched, but no one else seemed to react to the sulfurous scent Montoya knew came from the boy. Brandon gently held the tray handle in his hand and appeared to be unconsciously assuring that no piece of broken bread touched his fingers.

When all the boys completed their rounds, they returned to the rostrum, and the priests offered the bread to each deacon in turn. Montoya watched as Brandon hesitated, then took a piece. He lifted it to his open mouth and closed his mouth as if the bread had gone in. But Montoya saw. The bread turned black as it touched Brandon's lips and dropped like dust in an instant.

The deacons remained standing, heads bowed again, as the sacramental prayer over the water—the representation of the blood of Christ—was spoken. Again, Brandon took his tray, made his rounds, and returned without issue. Grasping his minuscule cup of water, Brandon brought it to lips and puffed out a quick breath. The water vaporized and Brandon continued the motion of partaking of the water.

Keeping his eyes on Brandon as the boy sat with his mother and brother, Montoya was able to set aside his distaste for the corny, whispered testimonies of children and their parents. The odor had faded but Montoya continued his vigil. At the end of the meeting, he shook an appropriate number of hands and was able to find the Smiths before they parted for their individual Sunday school classes.

"Hello, Sister Smith," Montoya said. "Brandon, David, good morning."

"Hello, President Montoya," Maddie said. "Thank you for being here."

"The duty and the pleasure are mine," he said. He released Maddie's hand and reached for Brandon's. "I was hoping to have a quick chat with your eldest, if I may?"

"You up for that, big guy?" Maddie said.

"Sure." Brandon accepted Montoya's hand as he spoke. "I don't mind missing deacon's quorum for a bit."

"I know you will be, but please be kind," Maddie said to Montoya. "He's still… well, I'm sure you can imagine."

"Yes, Sister, I can," Montoya said. With Brandon trailing a step behind, Montoya walked the short way to

Bishop Griffen's office, shaking a few more hands along the way, and closed the door once Brandon had entered.

"Thank you for coming with me. I know the last week, and from what I've heard, the last month or so, have been rather difficult."

"Yeah, well, you know." Brandon sat, toying with the sleeves of his suit coat, then tucking a wayward corner of bandage back beneath his collar. "Things happen. Is that what you want to talk about?"

"Yes and no. We don't have to talk about Bishop Griffen, if you don't want to. You know he and I were mission companions?"

"I think I heard my mom say that. Old friends, huh?"

"Older now than we were."

"I feel old sometimes."

"Do you?"

"Yeah, like during the day I just want to nap like those old guys you see on TV. Older than you, even."

"I understand. Let me ask you something else, please?"

"Uh-huh."

"Have you read your Bible or Book of Mormon lately?"

"I tried, but I got so tired and the books are so heavy."

"You haven't been doing any drugs, Brandon?"

"Gosh, no. Just the stuff they gave me at the hospital. But it's almost out and then maybe some Tylenol if Mom lets me."

"What kind of music do you like?"

"Imagine Dragons and Marshmallo. My friend Riley turned me on to them."

"You haven't felt like hurting yourself, have you, Brandon?"

"No. I hurt enough," Brandon said. He paused and closed eyes. Faintly, the odor Montoya had noticed during sacrament meeting returned. Brandon cleared his throat, lowering his voice. "I like this body, Rey. It suits me better than the last one."

"Ruin."

"I am here and he is mine." Brandon leapt from his chair and ran out of the office, leaving Montoya behind in a cloud of sulfur.

***

At sixty-four, Montoya's sprinting days were well behind him, but he maintained some of his youthful slenderness and was able to get out from behind Griffen's former desk without too much trouble. But he knew his age and knew he'd missed a few of his heart pills in the commotion of the last few days. He wouldn't be able to catch up to Brandon without risking harm to himself. But he knew where Maddie would be.

Straightening his suit and tie, finding a few vials of consecrated oil in a desk drawer, and putting on the calmest face he could muster, Montoya sauntered out of the office. No one milled about in the corridors or the vestibule, which meant Brandon had little chance to engage any other members. Montoya walked stiffly to the Relief Society meeting room, casually opened the door, and scanned for Maddie. She, along with the other women of the ward, turned toward the opening door. Montoya nodded at her and she stood. He didn't want to frighten her among her church sisters. His heart pounded with anticipation—he hoped just anticipation.

Neither said a word, other than to stop at the primary classes and ask Sister Christensen if she would mind having David over after the service ended. She agreed. Maddie gave David a hug and he whispered in her ear as she did.

"You're going to help Brandon." It was not a question. Montoya could hear the fear and determination in his voice despite the attempt at a low volume.

"Yes, baby," Maddie said. "We're going to help

Brandon."

"If I was old enough and had the Priesthood, I'd help, too," the boy said.

"You can pray," Montoya said. "Pray hard."

"I will." David let go of his mother and returned to his class. The children began singing his favorite song: "I Am a Child of God."

Lead me and guide me, too, Heavenly Father, Montoya thought.

***

Ruin guided Brandon without Brandon's permission. The boy did his best to influence the course of his own body, but he was no longer in control. His head pounded, tiny jackhammers digging through his skull from the inside. From one eye, he could see the streets of Blackhawk, a few people on the sidewalks or driving, but mostly empty as the town's Mormon majority were either still at home or still in church. The Walgreen's across the street from their meetinghouse was open, and the gas station kitty-corner, but the businesses on Main Street stood empty as Brandon's body flew past them.

Through his other eye, or perhaps just in his mind, Brandon saw fire again. He'd had enough of fire and tried to close his mind's eye against it. Whatever controlled his body wouldn't allow it. The flames subsided, but left a red tint on every image beyond the conflagration. Next, he saw a pair of twisted hands in front of him, as if he was looking at his own hands. And then a larger hand reached and grabbed him. His vision followed the hand up an arm and into a vaguely familiar face. The mouth of the man Brandon now saw moved, but Brandon couldn't make out the words. The man shook the arm he held, and his voice became louder, although Brandon felt it more than heard it. A floating sensation came over Brandon and he saw the full body of the man he couldn't hear as well as the body of a man who looked like one of the old photos he'd seen in his mom's genealogy books. He couldn't place the new face, but now recognized the face of the larger man. The Prophet Joseph Smith continued to hold the arm of the other man as Brandon floated between them.

He'd lost track of where he was being taken and momentarily everything felt unfamiliar. The bandages on his healing burns loosened beneath the sweat of running at full speed and Brandon silently begged to sit down. His body pushed forward, his legs pumping harder than before. He heard the tearing of his suit coat and saw his own hand grasp his tie, tug it loose and pull it over his head, leaving it on the ground. Brandon still couldn't tell exactly where he was and so returned his focus to the other eye. He didn't want to see what was there, but knew that if he watched carefully, he might find a way back to control.

***

"We need to stop at home first," Maddie said. She drove with Montoya, talking about the places Brandon might have run to. There's something in his room I need."

"Make it quick. We can't let him get too far."

She knew right where to go. The gold ring had barely left Brandon's hand after he'd been found at the house. He had to be fully sedated before the nurses could pry open his fingers enough to take the CTR ring out of his hand. The police photographed it, fingerprinted it, and—miraculously— let Brandon keep it. She'd watched him hold it a few times, practically worshiping it like Gollum in *The Lord of the Rings*. Other times, she saw him set it down and purposefully push it out of his sight while still respecting its presence. She didn't see him grab it before they left for church and when she entered his room, it was sitting on his nightstand. The green shield emblazoned with CTR faced away from the bed, making the engraving visible.

Samantha Robinson had gone missing when Maddie was in first grade. She'd seen the news and been warned about "stranger danger" by every adult she knew. Somehow, Samantha had ended up in that house, not just left there, but buried there. What if she had found the body instead of Brandon? She wished she'd never gone there, knowing that whatever had happened to her and could now be happening to Brandon was because she had to check out that stupid, old, god damned house.

She grabbed the ring and muttered a prayer that Samantha had found peace with Jesus.

***

Brandon saw Samantha not in the skeletal form in which he'd first met her, but as she had been before. Blackhawk had hung onto the 1980s for a few years into the 1990s and Samantha's tall bangs served as evidence of that. She wore jeans like Brandon had seen Randy wearing, but now the term "acid wash" came to him along with the image. Her jeans were tighter and led up to an equally tight green sweater with a silver B sewn on the front. The bottom hole of the letter framed the roaring lion mascot of Blackhawk High. Samantha wore the sleeves pushed up to her elbows and a Trapper Keeper folder bounced against her inner arm.

The image blinked and Brandon now saw Samantha from behind, same jeans on but with a light jacket, maybe over the sweater, he couldn't tell. He felt himself get excited watching her and saw a new set of hands reach down and adjust himself between the legs. He enjoyed the sensation as he knew the owner of the hands and eyes he used enjoyed it. He heard voices, but like before, he could not understand the words. Two bodies flanked him. He turned and saw Randy and Marlon, which meant the eyes he looked through belonged to Doug. He tried to look away as the scene sped up: Doug approaching Samantha alone, Doug taking her to his car, Doug opening the front door of the 600 North house only to see Marlon and Randy there waiting. The three men urging Samantha to the cellar. In one corner stood an easel with a blank canvas on it. On the floor a dark circle with a star in the center had been marked and candles sputtered at the tips of the star.

Samantha let her jacket fall to the ground as she stepped into the circle. Brandon, through Doug's eyes, saw Marlon and Randy take off their pants but not their black shirts. He felt himself do the same, followed by covering his head with some kind of hood. By the time the hood had been fit into place, Samantha had fully stripped, letting her CTR ring dangle between her breasts. Brandon had never seen a naked woman. The sight made him ill as much as it excited him. He wanted to look away, but couldn't. Then, after so much silence, a familiar voice spoke to him.

Too young for this, child? I will spare you from the physical relations of adults.

Darkness cut Brandon's vision but when his sight returned, he wished it hadn't.

Watch, now.

He loomed over Samantha, she still completely nude and he from the waist down. Doug's hands—his hands—held her throat in one and a knife in the other. Next to him kneeled Randy, holding the canvas. With each thrust of the knife, blood splattered onto Doug's torso and onto the canvas. The white became red and Brandon could see a picture emerging from the blood. Three men standing in one corner wearing dark shirts and hoods but no pants. In the foreground, a young woman, blonde like Samantha Robinson, on her knees and nude. Next to her a splotch of red seemed to pull in the rest of the blood red, becoming a muscular crimson body with a protruding erection.

In his head, Brandon screamed. He screamed enough to blot out any further visions of Doug, Samantha, or the hideous painting he knew had burned up with the rest of the house.

Quiet now. Just one more thing to show you…

No, Brandon thought. *I don't want to see anymore. I won't.*
You don't have a choice.

***

"Where do you think he went," Maddie asked as she got back in the car. "He wouldn't have gone back to that rubble, would he?"

"'I am Ruin,' you said while you were under its control," Montoya said. "From ruin it came, from ruin it was named. So why not to ruin it be returned?"

"I don't want to go back there."

"I know. But for your son, it should be the first place we check."

After buckling her seatbelt, Maddie folded her arms and bowed her head, as she had done since she was a child. Montoya followed her lead.

"Dear Father in Heaven," she prayed. "Watch over us as we search for Brandon. Whatever he might be doing right now, it's not his fault. Lord, show him Thy grace and lead us to him. In the name of Jesus Christ. Amen."

"Amen. Now floor it."

Floor it she did, getting honked at by one of her neighbors as they returned from church. She wouldn't let anything stop her from saving her son.

Chapter Fourteen: A Man Must Be Called

Police tape still surrounded the blackened property. The east wall stood taller than the rest of the house, it's 160-year-old sandstone reduced to piles of scorched brick. Every splinter of wood in the house had burned and ashes floated on the breeze like evil dandelion seeds. The entity inside Brandon looked for signs of its presence and found none. With Brandon's foot, it kicked at the rubble, angry that its home had been destroyed but joyous at the fulfillment of its name. It was free of the murdered woman's sacrifice but would need a new home when the current vessel deteriorated. *Why are we, the many, so jealous of this weak human flesh*, it thought. *It never lasts.*

A spike of pain rang through the body, and while slight compared to the torments of Hell, shocked the demon. The vessel had placed its foot over a nail and pushed down. Inside, the entity knew Brandon felt the pain, as well, and relished it. It picked up a handful of soot and rubbed it on its face. Another handful of ash went into its mouth, and it was good.

The demon scanned the ruins of the old house once more, then began walking south, leaving a trail of blood from its pierced foot. The oozing from its foot did not slow it down.

***

"There's nothing here," Montoya said, bracing himself as Maddie braked to a hard stop.

"No, but he would have come here first anyway, like you said," she said.

They exited the car, Montoya watching for on-lookers, Maddie looking for a sign that Brandon had been there. A variety of footprints were scattered across the grounds, the huge tread of firefighter boots mixed with tread marks from fire trucks and police cruisers. Some cradled small pools of water left over from the efforts to douse the home. One shallow print contained a tiny pool of bright, fresh blood. Nearby was a similar print, minus the blood. And then another matching print with another smear of blood.

"He was here; look!" Maddie said, directing Montoya to the spattered footprints.

"Then we follow."

***

The entity—Ruin—walked and ran, but didn't know where it headed. North, it knew and somewhat west, yes, but to where? It allowed itself to be guided by instinct. Soon it crossed beneath a white arch in disrepair. The asphalt road it had been running on narrowed into squared paths, the paths creating a grid as if it was just another Mormon pioneer settlement. Stone outcroppings loomed over shorter ones in various shapes and Ruin knew this could be a place of refuge, at least for a moment. It saw a door built into a granite façade and marched toward it. The injured foot of the vessel slowed it down some, seemed to deliberately scrape its sole on the ground, but Ruin plodded on.

Etchings of the Christ's symbol were visible among a smattering of the stone monuments, and a few held the symbol at their topmost points. Not as many as other places it had seen, but enough. They were pretty, it thought, but didn't keep it from touching some of them and tasting the names on its tongue. It felt a few names recoil from his connection to the other planes of existence, but none that shouted in triumph.

Reaching the door, Ruin sat the vessel down and smiled. It had done another horrible job, destroyed another wholesome family, and brought followers of Christ closer to losing faith. *Well done*, it thought. *Well done, servant.*

It closed the eyes of the vessel and found his host inside, not fighting like all others had before, but sitting in a dark corner of his mind, looking at a book. Its visage grabbed the flimsy book from the boy's hands. The rectangular book held several blank pages at the back and other pages filled with photos of its vessel and the vessel's family. Ruin spat on a photo of the vessel's mother and did its best to slam the thick paper covers together. On the front cover, Ruin read *Brandon's Book of Remembrance.*

You'll remember nothing but torture, fleshworm, Ruin made its visage say.

The vessel, Brandon, said nothing. He folded his arms and bowed his head, never looking at Ruin's image.

***

Maddie ran, head down with her eyes on the red tracks Brandon had left for her. Behind her, Montoya did his best to keep up, yelling when he thought Maddie might be hit by an oncoming car or run into a garbage can in the street. He saw the gates of Blackhawk Cemetery first. The flaking paint of the gate contrasted with the green lawns beyond it. He saw the few cross-topped headstones and the dark bumps of the flatter stones. A few feet in, Maddie stopped and Montoya finally joined her. He wheezed breaths and his heart hammered in his chest.

A stain of red marked the path where Maddie stood. She panned the cemetery from the spot Brandon had been moments before.

Montoya's eyes went to the fresh mound of earth under which Blaine Griffen's body lay. *And there it shall remain until the trumpets sound and we are perfected in the resurrection*, Montoya thought. *I'll be joining you soon, brother.*

***

Had she lingered on Griffen's burial plot, as Montoya did, Maddie would have lost the trail of blood that had led them here. She didn't spare an extra glance at the section where members of her own family were interred. This time did not belong to the past and those ancestors, but to the future of her child.

The bloody trail ended at the edge of one section of lawn. The well-kept grass masked more footprints and swallowed any drops of blood Brandon may have left. She knelt on the edge of the grass, searching for a clue to Brandon's direction. In the distance, she saw a shadow against the door of the small mausoleum in one corner of the cemetery. It wavered and looked as if it was growing, then shrank to the size and shape of a small man. Her son. As she began to stand, hands fell on her shoulders, keeping her in a penitent position.

"We need to do something first," Montoya said.

***

In the shadow of death, Ruin made Brandon see more than the boy wanted. Brandon watched a small parade of people look at the cellar painting, but none who touched it. He saw his mother walk down the cellar steps, hesitate, and continue toward the painting. Her fingers reached out and he felt the tips as if she were caressing his cheek and not canvas. After that, he saw her burning, tormented, her skin crawling with fire and insects.

Through the eyes of Ruin, Brandon saw Joseph Smith again, kneeling in the Sacred Grove where the prophet had experienced his first vision. He had always imagined the grove to be denser, darker, with more trees. And then he saw that, no, this was not the prophet like he had seen before but someone pretending to be the prophet. Behind the actor, an armored battalion of angels stood on the wall of the Manti temple—in Utah not New York—and the storm above the temple formed from clouds and lightning but also black and red demons without earthly hosts, screaming at the silent angels standing guard. The demons in the sky bellowed horrible threats at the angels and even at Ruin, jealous that it was in a body and they were not. They howled at their co-conspirator because they could not be happy for it. Satisfaction is denied all demons, even successful ones. They laughed from above as Ruin, in Maddie's body, flailed among the faithful and was then carted off.

The angelic host remained still.

New images went by quickly: Montoya and Griffen near Maddie, Ruin being launched out of her, flung back into the painting instantaneously, only to be touched by Brandon seconds later and released again. Brandon watched Bishop Griffen fall into the flames not from above as his memory told him he should but from below, from a small part of Ruin that would be buried under the rubble of the house and would sink back into Hell to await the return of the rest of its incorporeal being.

Another glimpse of his own home and room came to Brandon, from a low angle. He sensed movement, but saw no people. More images came that felt familiar; recent, but unplaceable.

Here we sit. You twist inside this body as my disease spreads through it. Many bodies over millennia have I crumbled. I brought down souls centuries before your prophet was born. Yours is another mark in my record.

Soul-Brandon, older even than Brandon's body according to a lesson he'd heard one Sunday, listened but did not submit.

We many were there, too, meat. You are not special.

Looking up from his prayer, Brandon smiled at the entity.

"Yes, I am. I am a child of God," Brandon said. "And He has sent me here."

***

"I can't do it alone," Montoya said. "I can't do the blessings alone. It's not only that I feel the strain on my heart, but it takes two, sometimes more, but at least two people with the Priesthood, especially for something as big as this."

"I don't have the Priesthood," Maddie said. "We don't ordain women. And if, if we did, I'm…I'm not worthy."

"I can hear your repentance now. We'll worry about the rest later. But we must be quick. Pray your repentance, Sister."

Gulping down a breath, Maddie began her address to Heavenly Father, confessing her disappointments, her failures, her desire to have been a better wife and to be a better mother. Tears streamed down her cheeks, wetting the grass beneath her. Montoya's hands didn't leave her shoulders. As she prayed, she heard whistling, a Primary children's song. She started to stand again, but Montoya held her in place.

"It's Brandon! He's whistling so we can find him," she said.

"It could be the demon, whistling for us to rush in unprepared. The Lord hears your prayer and forgives you. And I know He will forgive me if this is the wrong decision. We need to be armed for spiritual battle."

Montoya lifted his hands from her shoulders and placed them on her head. She felt the familiar weight of them and missed the hands of his companion.

"Madeline Patricia Knight Smith, by the authority of the Melchizedek Priesthood which I hold, I confer upon you the Aaronic Priesthood, restored to this earth to the prophet Joseph Smith and ordain you to the office of priest, granting you all keys and authority to perform the duties of the priesthood in accordance to the gospels of our Father in Heaven. I bless you that this conference will prepare you for further blessings and to serve as part of the armor of God. In the name of Jesus Christ. Amen.

"Amen," Maddie said. "Let's go."

"It's not enough," Montoya said, his breathing becoming shallow. "Father in Heaven, again I beseech you that if there were another way, we would have done it."

The whistling grew louder, but Maddie felt a patience she did not sense before. She focused on images of Jesus, more comforting paintings than the one that started all this trouble. Jesus with His hands out, palms up, walking among the clouds and surrounded by trumpeting angels. Christ cradling a black sheep as other white sheep milled around his feet. Christ with a whip, scattering the money changers at the temple in Jerusalem.

With his hands laid upon her, Montoya began the next confirmation.

"Madeline Patricia Knight Smith, having the authority of the Melchizedek Priesthood, which was restored to the earth by the ancient apostles Peter, James, and John to the prophet Joseph Smith, I confirm upon you the very same Melchizedek Priesthood and ordain you to the office of Elder. With this authority you shall hold the keys to the priesthood to administer to the sick, to consecrate and anoint sacred oil, and to seal anointings on those who are in need.

"Maddie, as the head of your household, you are the protector of your family's faith, defender of your children's morality, and forger of the straight and narrow path for your sons. With this new authority bestowed upon you by God our Father in Heaven, you shall wage a holy war against temptation, against demonic influence, and lead the battle to dispossess the children of God from the spawn of Satan and those spirits who desire mortal bodies but were denied them in the pre-existence. Your faith and perseverance are needed now, Maddie. By the power of God, His Son Jesus, and the Holy Ghost, I bless you with the strength to cast out evil spirits as Jesus did in the New Testament and as Joseph Smith did for your ancestor Newel Knight…"

Maddie had listened reverently to Montoya's words, but a screech of pain blasted across the cemetery when Montoya said she had an ancestor who had been possessed. She wanted to rush toward the scream and finish this, but Montoya's hands held her head in place.

"Your family, Maddie, has had a history with evil spirits. With this priesthood authority confirmed upon you, you shall be a force to end the affliction in your lives and for your sons. I say this all in the name of Jesus Christ. Amen."

Silence. No whistling, no screeching. Not even a breeze. And then, from Maddie, "Amen."

Opening her eyes, Maddie saw the path to the mausoleum as if it had been illuminated for her. A breeze swirled up again and once more carried the tune of Brandon's whistle to her ears. "Can we go now?" she said.

Chapter Fifteen: Toil and Sorrow

Inside his head, Brandon began whistling "I Am a Child God." Ruin lashed out at him. The demon tried to seal Brandon's lips shut by wrapping a leather band over his mouth. When the demon let go of the ends of the band, it fell from Brandon's face. Ruin grabbed Brandon by the jaw and produced a bone needle and thread made from its own sable hair. When Ruin tried to pierce the skin below Brandon's lip, the needle broke.

Brandon continued to whistle.

No one can hear you, meatbag. You aren't anywhere for them to find.

No, Brandon answered without having to speak. *But you are.*

Out of the darkness surrounding them, Ruin constructed a barrier around Brandon. Building was not its nature, but so be it.

***

"I believe we follow the whistling," Montoya said, lifting his hands from Maddie's head. In his pounding heart and wrenching gut, Montoya knew bestowing the Priesthood upon Maddie was the only way to win this day, but what it would cost him, he couldn't know. Ex-communication from the only earthly thing he loved as much as his departed wife? Perhaps. He would deal with that when the time came. For

171

now, he silently prayed for forgiveness and strength. Ahead of him, Maddie followed a trail only she could see, but they both could hear.

The shadows pulled in around the small tomb, clouding it in darkness and leaving the rest of the cemetery sunlit and healthy. A rancid odor attacked Montoya and he looked around for a fallen bird's nest and the rotten eggs it must contain, then remembered the odor that permeated the shack in Chile and had risen from Brandon during the sacrament. "We are close, Maddie. Be careful. These devils have many tricks."

She waved a hand at him and he noticed a gold ring on her finger. Another flash of her hand and he saw the green CTR shield of the ring. *Even we have our talismans, he thought. No crosses, no saints' medals, no prayers in a foreign language. We have a ring and the power of Almighty God.*

He walked and prayed. Like a good Mormon, a Latter-day Saint, Montoya prayed only to God the Father in the name of Jesus Christ. After his conversion, he would slip and pray to Joseph Smith, thinking him to be a patron saint like St. Paul, one to be prayed to for certain things. He learned and now prayed for the strength of the prophet to cast out devils in the name of Christ. When this was over, he might indeed reach out to President Ballard and have a conversation. He'd even take the not-so-young Taysom with him.

That is, if his heart settled down long enough to finish this work.

***

Behind her, Maddie could hear the strain in Montoya's breathing as he muttered his prayers. His prayers didn't obscure the sound of whistling from the mausoleum, though. Her path was direct now. She didn't need to look for the drops of blood or the patches of grass that were slightly stomped down. Her body, in pain for so long, ached but felt lighter. Her skin vibrated with power, so different than the squirming sensation she'd had in that house. The house was gone, the horrible painting destroyed. Her son remained, now fighting the demon on his own. She would not let him suffer as long as she had.

Nearing the tomb, her sight dead-set on the door, Maddie tripped. She tumbled forward but caught herself before slamming her head into a gravestone. She screamed and tipped back onto her butt, scuttling away from the stone she nearly brained herself upon. Her back bumped into Montoya's legs and she turned into him, looking away from the headstone.

BELOVED MOTHER
Madeline Patricia Smith
Born 12-27-1983
Died 8-5-2018

Her epitaph was flanked by those of her sons, each with the same date of death.

"It's a trick, Maddie," Montoya said. "A lie. No one is dying today."

"I just," Maddie started. "I know. It—that thing—lies. But it wants Brandon, it still wants me. It would take David next, if it could. We have to stop it."

"Then what are we waiting for?" Montoya said, pointing at the mausoleum. The door creaked open and the whistling grew louder.

"Brandon!" Maddie yelled. She got her feet under her and sprinted to the tomb.

"Heavenly Father be with us now. In the name of your Son Jesus. Amen," Montoya said, following Maddie into the tomb.

***

The thick stone door groaned shut behind Maddie and Montoya, shutting out the limited light available. Maddie closed her eyes, trying to pick up the whistle again. She heard it, but the pitch had deepened, and the tune changed. No longer did "I Am a Child of God" ring in her ears, but something darker. Something from her teen years that brought up shame in her, a revulsion at a sinister rock and roll parody of something she was meant to cherish by a band she and her friends adored. And then it stopped. Maddie closed and opened her eyes several times before adjusting enough to see the parameters of the tomb: a small walkway, two stomach-high, body-wide platforms on each side, a runner of reinforced stained glass just below the slope of the ceiling. The glass let in some light, but the tomb remained dark.

A small movement to her right caused Maddie to spin and knock Montoya down from his post behind her. He gasped as he landed, and Maddie thought she heard something crack. She reached her hands out to him to help him up and saw his face darken as another shadow grew behind her.

"Maddie," Montoya croaked. "Watch out!"

She let go of his hands and he plopped back down on the floor, the cracking sounds twice as loud as before. As she let go, she ducked, avoiding swooping arms that sought to capture her.

"Hug me, mother," came a voice from Brandon's mouth, but it was not his voice. "Give your boy a hug, sow."

She rolled as far to the right as she could, getting behind Brandon but leaving him between herself and Montoya. "Where's my son?"

"He'ssss in heeerre with usssss," the being using Brandon's body said. "We sssssspeak like sssnakessss to sssscare the fakessssss." The thing's eyes homed in on Montoya and smiled. "Boo!"

Montoya sat still, pain radiating from his tailbone, but offered no other reaction.

"Why aren't you scared, false priest," the entity said,

grabbing Montoya under his chin and squeezing his cheeks. "Or are you too afraid to speak?"

"I shall fear no evil," Montoya spat out.

"Your missionary friends are still burning. They lusted after the girl and burn for the sin in their hearts before they died."

Montoya didn't answer but also didn't allow himself to watch Maddie unscrewing a bottle of consecrated oil behind the body of her son. He avoided watching her raise her arm and begin to tip the bottle so that oil would fall on Brandon's head.

"Their sins were paid for, as are mine, by the Lord Jesus Christ whom we serve this day."

The oil poured slowly, but after the first drop, Maddie became less careful. She tipped the vial over and dumped the anointing oil on Brandon's head. The golden liquid sluiced through Brandon's hair, leaving behind trails of smoke. Scalding his scalp, the oil left black patches of skin bubbling, then clearing as if instantly healed. As it ran across Brandon's head, the oil seemed to multiply, becoming greater than what Maddie poured from the small vial. Some foamed in Brandon's hair but more poured down over his ears and onto his forehead.

The entity screeched, flailing Brandon's arms around his head, trying to wipe the oil way before it could reach Brandon's eyes. It jumped onto one platform and then to the other. As it leapt, it smashed Brandon's body into the ceiling, then fell, landing again between Maddie and Montoya.

"Grab him," Montoya said. "We have to anoint the oil and seal it. I will do the anointing. When you seal it, you have to use the same prayer but say 'seal.'"

Maddie nodded, unsure if he saw her, and grabbed Brandon about the waist as his body's flailing slowed from the ceiling impact. As Montoya slowly rose, Maddie lifted Brandon onto one of the platforms. Montoya took his place beside her.

"For now," Montoya said, "follow my lead. Focus on your son and the Son of God." He gently took Maddie's hands and placed them on Brandon's head. He placed his own so that the edge of his right hand pressed against the edge of Maddie's left. He saw the gold CTR ring on her finger. "We have chosen the right," he whispered.

"What?" Maddie said.

"Nothing. I will anoint the oil now. What is your son's full name?"

"Brandon Keith Smith."

A whistle floated on the air for moment, not the harsh one, but the one that led them here.

"Brandon Keith Smith…" Montoya began. He prayed for the oil to be anointed just as he had done for Maddie mere days before. The body beneath their hands shook and the sulfurous stench permeated the enclosed space. Montoya finished the anointing and looked at Maddie next to him. "No matter what, do not take your hands off his head. If he shakes, if he looks like he will roll off the platform, if it looks like his whole head is going to twist around, do not remove your hands."

"His head…that…that doesn't really happen," Maddie said.

"Sister…excuse me, Elder Smith, be prepared for anything." In another life, Montoya might have laughed, but solemnity took precedence. "I do mean anything. Begin the sealing, Elder."

"Brandon Keith Smith, by the authority of the Holy Melchizedek Priesthood which we hold…" Brandon's eyes opened as she prayed. They were not his deep blue but rather a diseased, blood-shot yellow. He blinked and his eyes were red. Maddie closed her own eyes and continued the sealing. "We seal this anointing oil upon you so that you may be healed of the sickness inside you. In your torment…" Tears began to form in Maddie's eyes. They fell from her face and landed on Brandon. His skin, dark with the remnants of ash he was forced to swallow and that had covered him, washed clean where his mother's tears touched. "In your toil and sorrow, your suffering, be comforted in being a child of God. My child, my son, you belong to Him and someday you'll be with Heavenly Father and Jesus. We bless you now that the day you sit with Christ not be today."

Brandon's mouth opened, spewing ash into the air. Then he screamed, but Maddie couldn't tell if it was her son or the demon. Above their heads, the stained glass shattered, sending colored flakes of glass into the air, mixing with the ash. Next to Maddie, Montoya began to cough. Maddie checked and saw ash land on his skin and turn to flies. The flies then returned to the cloud above them to fight the splintered glass. He looked at her and shook his head, then nodded back at Brandon without a word. Maddie clenched her jaw and continued the blessing.

"Brandon, nothing happening now is your fault. Nothing that has happened to your family is your fault. Any sins you may have committed can be forgiven in the blood of Christ. The Lord and your mother will always love you."

Beneath Brandon, the platform began shaking again. A crack in the concrete formed at his ear and split down, across the floor, and into the opposite platform. The crack split the concrete, revealing a deteriorating casket around a steel shell. Bones rattled inside the shell, but the steel did not split open.

"Now, Brandon, with the Priesthood power granted us and in the name of Jesus Christ, the only begotten son of our Father in Heaven, we command the entity inside you who calls itself Ruin to be gone from your body, your mind, and your spirit. Your work here is not done but the work of this demonic influence ends now."

The ash and glass cloud dispersed, some raining to the ground, some floating out through the holes left by the broken glass. More light entered the tomb. Maddie could see her son, arms stiff at his sides now, barely breathing. She wanted nothing more than to hug him to her, to kiss his forehead and tell him he was a good boy. But the blessing had not concluded.

"Brandon, by the authority of the Melchizedek Priesthood and the blessing of Heavenly Father, we cast out the demons inside you and banish them to the realm of those who sided with Lucifer in the pre-existence. We pray this all in the name of Jesus Christ. Amen."

"Ame—" Montoya started. The ground beneath him shook, sending pain through his injured tailbone. His heart jackhammered in his chest. "Amen."

The crack spread through the opposite wall of the mausoleum and across the ceiling. Maddie removed her left hand from Brandon's head to steady Montoya. As her fingers grazed his shoulder, a slab of concrete crashed down from the ceiling onto the shoulder where Maddie's hand had been reaching. Montoya fell to the ground with only a subdued groan and was silent.

"Mom," she heard, her right hand still on the crown of Brandon's head. "What's happening? Where are—"

"Nnnnnoooo!" A second voice, one all too familiar to Maddie howled from Brandon's mouth. "One must be mine. We are many and we shall see you in ruins!"

"Not my son, you bastard!" Maddie screamed. She raised her hand off Brandon's head and swung down to strike his face. Before her oil-stained palm could connect with her son's face, it stopped and another howl came from the few inches between Brandon's cheek and Maddie's palm. She closed her hand around the solidifying darkness and yanked. She tugged a shadow the size of a large man out of Brandon's mouth and threw it to the ground.

"I cast thee out, demon," she yelled. "I cast thee out in the name of Jesus."

The shadow flattened and rose to the cracked ceiling. As it touched the roof, sparks trickled from it and caught the roof of the vault on fire.

"Mom?" Brandon's own voice, weak and tired, but his own voice, called to her again.

"Son, we need to get out this place. And we need to help him." With one arm, she hoisted Brandon off the platform, then moved the concrete chunk away from Montoya and gathered him by the uninjured arm. With the weight of three people, if not their strength, she pushed open the door. She sat them down a few yards away from the mausoleum and watched the fire roar for a moment then peter out on its own, the leftovers of Ruin, leaving only smoke.

"Mom. Mom, do we need to call someone?" Brandon asked.

"They'll see the smoke and send someone. Just lay down for a moment."

Maddie followed her own advice, laying her head on a stone that cooled her warm cheek. She smiled at seeing a carving of Jesus cradling the smiling face of a young child and thanked the Lord for her own sons.

All is Well

The redhead wearing the long-sleeved T-shirt and black gloves knocked on the door for a third time. No one had answered yesterday, and no one was answering today. He knew someone must be home when a curtain on the second floored fluttered and he briefly saw the face of an adolescent boy. He didn't want to pound on the door or start yelling like a maniac in this quiet neighborhood. He couldn't ask anyone about the family that lived there because all the houses were new. A mile away, in the neighborhood he'd grown up in, he could have knocked on any door and known the person behind it.

Well, maybe ten years ago. Blackhawk had changed, he knew. New businesses. New families. New, new, new. His own life had changed. Nobody wanted an anthology series anymore. They wanted hour-long horror dramas with comic book witches and comic book zombies. Hell, he thought, people were even getting tired of the zombies.

But they also wanted—they, in this case, meaning his producers, the people who funded his existence—reality horror. True stories of haunted houses, haunted prisons, haunted lives. He pitched his own story and Darcy, the new head of production at the streaming service that had taken over *Graveyard Paradise* before canceling it, laughed at him.

What's so scary about Utah? Other than a bunch of backward, white Mormons and their weird Mormon shit? Now that's scary.

They don't like to be called Mormons anymore, Darcy. It's just Latter-day Saints now. And trust me, I can find some weird shit if you want it.

She'd laughed at first, when he told her about a house burning down the day before a small fire broke out at the cemetery in his hometown. When he added that the body of a woman missing since the 1990s had been found in the ruins of the house, she stopped laughing.

Bring me treatments for four episodes, Darcy had said. *And they'd better be good.*

Peter Toombs returned to Blackhawk, not looking for his own story this time, but for others. Maddie Smith and her boys had moved to a new neighborhood on the other side of I-15, but no one would answer the door. The church archivist he'd spoken to—Taylor? No, Taysom—told him a wild story about two dispossessions in town, a mother and her son.

"Dispossession?" Toombs asked.

"Yeah," Taysom said. "Like exorcisms. The real deal." Taysom shared the obituaries of Bishop Blaine Griffen and Stake President Rey Montoya who had been mission companions. Griffen had died in the house fire and Montoya a few weeks later from complications due to injuries and a heart attack. Now Toombs had a notepad with Montoya's story and Maddie Smith's old address.

Getting the new one proved more difficult, but Peter did it. He just wished someone would answer the damn door. He stepped off the ledge, thinking he'd come back again tomorrow. Halfway down the sidewalk, he heard the door open.

"Why are you wearing gloves? It's July," said the voice of a boy behind him. He turned slowly, not wanting to startle the boy.

"You must be Brandon Smith," Toombs said, thinking the boy looked small for thirteen.

"No, I'm…" the boy paused.

"David? Younger brother, right?"

The boy started to nod, then stopped. He reached one hand out and curled his finger in the "come here" motion. The other hand held a stained and faded piece of paper with an old house on it. Toombs walked the few steps back to the door and the boy motioned for him to bend down so he could whisper in his ear.

Toombs crouched, expecting to be told the boy wasn't allowed to talk to strangers. He waited for it, ready to be turned away. His eyes drifted from the boy's to the house on the sheet of paper and back to the boy.

"I am…Ruin, and we are many."

THE END

Afterword

You're still here? Good. I have just a little bit more to say. Thanks for sticking around.

If you've turned here before reading the book, please stop. I do it, too; I'm always interested in the writer's inside secrets and maybe a peek into their process. You could call what I'm about to say a spoiler. While I'm at it, I should suggest you read CRY DOWN DARK first, but you don't have to. If you haven't, you'll want to go back and meet Peter Toombs from about a dozen years before the events of TELL NO MAN. You don't have to, but it will help you understand how this book ends.

CRY DOWN DARK is a book by a much younger man than the one who wrote TELL NO MAN, even though their publication dates aren't as far apart as their fictional events. The book in your hands took less than two years to write, compared to the decade CRY DOWN DARK took. The more I do this, the faster I get. I'd like to say "the better I get" but I will leave that up to you, reader.

I never set out to write a sequel, and TELL NO MAN isn't exactly that. It's more like an anthology entry. Something you'd see on Toombs' TV show *Graveyard Paradise*. But I have a secret for you (and this is why you should stop here and read the book first, if you've continued after the first warning). Maddie, Peter, Brandon, and David have more to do. We'll learn more about Blackhawk's history and maybe—maybe—learn about those weirdos up in Bern and why they were being weird. I don't want to give away too much, but I will say that you won't have to wait another four years to find out. Barring the end of the world, that is.

I imagine you want to know more about this story, right? If you've read either of my collections, you've seen those little snippets of how stories came to be. There were tears and sweat, but I don't think any actual blood was spilt to get us here.

This started when I was nine. You can read about that in the essay "Street View" in THE PRIVATE LIVES OF NIGHTMARES, so I'm not going over that again here. What I will tell you is that I saw THE EXORCIST late at night with my sister and two of her friends when I was 14. I remember how freaked out my sister and one of her friends were on our drive back home. Those are moments that stick with me and are why I do what I do.

I love that movie and the book that inspired it. There are so many exorcism books and movies and I've read and watched as many as possible. But they are mostly rooted in Catholicism, as if Catholics are the only people dealing with demons. I knew that not to be true. So the two words I kept throwing around were Mormon exorcists. As in, "Hey, T.J., what are you working on?"

"Mormon exorcists."

"Is that a thing?" would be the inevitable reply, because no one knew any better.

"It is in my book," I would say.

I am, however, a constant researcher. I regularly plugged my keywords into the databases and received no results. Then, one day, WHAM! Dr. Stephen Taysom's scholarly essay on the history of exorcism in the Church of Jesus Christ of Latter-day Saints popped up and my book instantly became more valid. A few emails here and there and

I had so much more to add. I had the power of witnessed truth to combine with my own know history.

And then I had a new twist. As I was finishing the book, my eldest uncle passed away. I drove nine hours to my hometown for the funeral. While there, I took pictures of some of the places that inspired TELL NO MAN. And one of my cousin's told me a story of his father's time in the mission field. That story is in here, too. I finished the draft during that week. I won't regale you with the adventures of submitting and waiting on other people between then and now. That's a bit more inside baseball for the other writers out there.

This book is even more Utah than CRY DOWN DARK is. I'm in a phase of reckoning with the places of my upbringing in a way that I did not expect. The truth is that I never anticipated returning to my fictional version of where I grew up. Now, however, more than half of the newer fiction I've written is set there. I've found myself remaking the world of my youth into something for you to engage with. I hope you find a home here, too.

So here we are, at the end of another journey together. Peter, Maddie, Brandon, and David will see you again in BLACKHAWK (as I have tentatively titled the next book).

Thank you, again, for hanging out in my head and reading this book. Your support means the world to me.

TJT
November 19, 2020
Kennewick, Washington

About the Author

T.J. Tranchell was born on Halloween and grew up in Utah. He has previously published the novella *Cry Down Dark* and the collections *Asleep in the Nightmare Room* and *The Private Lives of Nightmares* with Blysster Press. He has been a grocery store janitor, a college English and journalism instructor, an essential oils warehouse worker, a reporter, and a fast food grunt. He holds a Master's degree in Literature from Central Washington University and attended the Borderlands Press Writers Boot Camp in 2017. He currently lives in Washington State with his wife and son. Follow him at www.tjtranchell.net.

Also by T.J. Tranchell:

CRY DOWN DARK

ASLEEP IN THE NIGHTMARE ROOM

THE PRIVATE LIVES OF NIGHTMARES

ELEGY & ETUDE (eBook exclusive)

GIVE: AN ANTHOLOGY OF ANATOMICAL
ENTRIES (co-edited with Michelle Kilmer)

CPSIA information can be obtained
at www.ICGtesting.com
Printed in the USA
BVHW061655170322
631762BV00013B/1359

9 780578 827599